DON'T SCREAM 2

BLAIR DANIELS

My Confession, The Hat, I Found My Doppelganger on Facebook, and *Ice Road Trucker* were originally published by Thought Catalog at www.thoughtcatalog.com

Two Pinocchios, The Halloween Mask, and *The Haunting of Room 812* written and edited by Blair Daniels and Craig Groshek, in collaboration with Chilling Tales for Dark Nights, based on a concept created by Craig Groshek.

Siren Song written in collaboration with Chilling Tales for Dark Nights, as part of a planned collaboration with a singer-songwriter.

CONTENTS

MY CONFESSION

"Forgive me, Father, for I have sinned."
My voice shook as I spoke.
"It has been two years since my last confession."
"Go on, my daughter, and tell me your sins."
The priest's voice was low, quiet. Unfamiliar. That was by design – I'd driven 20 miles from my apartment, to a church in the middle of woods. It was easier that way. I took in a deep breath, but only a squeak came out.

Get it over with, I told myself. *Just say it.*

"Father, I'm guilty of gossip. Jealousy." The venial sins came out first, as they always did. It was almost easy to confess them. "And..."

My heart beat faster. My hands grew sweaty, slipping against the wood. I stared at the divider between us. White, cloth mesh. The priest's dark outline, on the other side.

"I did something terrible, a year ago."
Silence.

The kneeler bit into my legs. The stuffy heat pressed into me. *He has to accept my confession. Has to absolve me of my sins. Right? As long as I am genuinely, heartily sorry... which I am.* The mesh swam before my eyes; the shadow behind it shifted.

"I hit someone."

Once I'd lanced the wound, it all came bursting out of me. "I knew I had too much to drink. I knew I shouldn't have been driving. But I did. I sat behind that wheel, started my car, and —"

"Who was it, my daughter?"

His voice was surprisingly calm. No scream, no gasp, no groan of horror. I wondered briefly how many confessions he'd heard like this. Confessions past the normal realm of jealousy, anger, infidelity, theft.

How many murders had been confessed within these walls.

"I don't know. That—that's the worst part, Father. I just kept driving. I didn't... even stop." My voice cracked. Tears burned in my eyes. "I didn't check if they were still alive. Didn't call an ambulance. Didn't..."

"I understand, my daughter."

It was out. I'd told him everything. The tears rolled down my cheeks as I sobbed. Gaining composure, I said in a shaky voice: "Those are my sins, Father, and I am so sorry."

Silence.

It stretched into seconds, then minutes. The hot air pressed into me. My knees ached. Finally, I spoke. "Aren't you going to absolve me, Father?"

His voice came from the other side, loud and clear. "I'm afraid I can't do that."

"What? Why not?"

"Because I'm not a priest."

Horror thundered through me. "What do you mean, you're not a priest?"

No reply.

Who is he? A police officer? A man, waiting to do something terrible to me? Somebody... I lifted myself up from the kneeler, legs shaking, and peered around the divider.

I froze.

No one was there.

"What the hell?" I whispered. "Wherever you are, I'm going to —"

"Kill me?"

The voice came from behind me. I reeled around – a shadow flickered across the mesh, now on the other side. Where I'd just been kneeling.

I immediately ran over to the other side. But the kneeler was empty.

"Where are you?" I yelled.

"Everywhere," the voice echoed back.

In a panic, I ran to the door. Grabbed the knob. Turned it as hard as I could.

Locked.

"Let me out!" I screamed. The doorknob slipped and slid under my sweaty fingers. "Please, let me out!"

"No."

The voice was low and raspy – right in my ear. I whipped around. Nothing there. Just that vague silhouette, behind the cloth mesh. It was standing, now. As if, at any second, it would dart out and grab me.

"Help me!" I screamed, banging my fists against the door. "Please! Help!"

"You know what you did."

The voice seemed to come from every direction. Echoing, reverberating, growing louder and louder in overlapping whispers.

"You deserve this."

I threw my entire body against the door. It shook underneath me. *Thump.* I reeled back and threw my body against it again.

"Nothing can save you," it continued. *"You are beyond redemption. Worthless."*

"No!" I screamed, throwing my body against the door again. But I was weaker, this time. The guilt pulled me down like a weight of lead. "No... please..."

"Even if you get out that door, I will follow you. Wherever you go, I will be there."

The voice was dark and low. The shadow was pressed up against the mesh, now. It looked wrong – misshapen, twisted, different. Like something *trying* to look human.

"No!" I screamed and flung my body against the door.

It flew open.

I fell onto the floor. Coughing. Gasping. Spluttering.

"Are you alright?" a voice asked.

A priest stood over me. He extended a hand. Slowly, I climbed to my feet. I glanced back at the confessional — the room was empty. The shadow was gone.

I wanted to run. Out the door, into the parking lot, into my car. I wanted to drive and drive, until I was miles away from this place.

Miles away from what I did.

But no matter where I went – *it* would follow me. It would flicker across my rearview mirror on the open road. It would live in the mist on the hotel bathroom mirror. It would lie in the spare bed, roiling and twisting under the sheets, as I lay wide awake.

"I will follow you anywhere."

Raspy whispers filled my ears. A shadow flit at the corners of my vision. But I forced myself to look away. Forced myself not to listen.

I locked eyes with the priest.

"Father... I need to make a confession."

THE HAT

Grace always wore a hat to school.

Even in 90*F weather, she had that knitted, black beanie pulled down to her eyes. Rain or shine, hot or cold — always the hat.

It wasn't long before the rumors started. Since she was new, the rumors were especially cruel. "I bet she's bald," Marie said, watching Grace sit alone at the lunch table.

"No, I've seen some blonde hair poke out," I said. "She's not blonde."

"Maybe it's a style thing. Like goth or something," Marie replied.

"Hey. Don't bring us into this," Cara shouted from the end of the table, twirling a lock of dyed-black hair.

"Maybe her head just gets really cold. She could have a medical condition –"

"No. I've got it." Lara, the nerd of our little group, leaned forward. Her brown eyes gleamed with excitement behind her glasses. "It's a psychological experiment. This is exactly what she wants us to do. Focus on it, form theories about it, obsess over it. It's brilliant, actually. I bet she got Mr. Hernandez to sign off on it." Her fist slammed into the table. "Dammit, she's totally going to get an A in psych –"

"Stop it," Marie said, rolling her eyes. "Not everyone is obsessed with grades like you."

After lunch was Algebra 2. It went terribly, as usual, and I made a fool out of myself when Mr. Giordano called on me. I walked back to my locker in a foul mood, when I heard a voice call out behind me.

"Hey, Clara!"

It was Grace.

I'd never really seen her up close before. She was pretty, in a delicate sort of way; pale skin, pale blue eyes, tufts of blonde hair sticking out from underneath her hat. She wore lipstick, but no other makeup – a refreshing look, compared to the rest of the girls at school.

"I saw you get that question wrong," she started. "Sine is opposite over hypotenuse –"

"So?" I asked, bristling.

"Sorry, I didn't mean – I just wanted to help." She passed me a piece of paper. "This mnemonic helped me a lot. I thought it might help you for the test."

She gave me a small smile and walked away.

I watched as she disappeared down the hallway, and felt a pang of dread. Something about the shape of her head looked... wrong, somehow. The contours, and the shadows they created, looked out of place.

That's when I realized the truth.

She wears the hat because she has some sort of deformity. And here we are — laughing at her, mocking her. She must feel awful.

I felt rotten inside.

After that, I never talked about Grace at the lunch table. She was a nice person. Not only did she help me, but she also ignored the derisive laughs, the pointed fingers, when any other teenager would have fired right back.

We should have looked up to her, not made fun of her.

Days, then weeks, went by. Every day, Grace wore that black beanie on her head. But each time, it grew a little less shocking, a little more normal. The others slowly got used to it. We didn't talk about it anymore. Things were getting back to normal.

Then it all went to shit when we got the substitute teacher.

"I'm Mrs. Chang." The chalk scraped against the board as she wrote her name in fine cursive. "I'm your substitute teacher for U.S. History. We'll be starting with World War II, so please open your textbooks to page 264." She turned around and faced the class.

Her eyes fell on Grace.

"No hats in class," she said.

Grace's eyes widened. She went pale. The rest of the class broke into hushed whispers. All the other teachers had just grown used to it. Or were sympathetic to the fact she was the new kid, and let it slide.

Not Mrs. Chang. "Well, what are you waiting for? Take it off," she said, with an annoyed chuckle. "*Now.*"

"I can't," Grace replied, in a small voice.

My heart pounded in my chest. Grace didn't deserve this. Never.

"You can't take off your hat, huh?" Mrs. Chang paced through the rows of desks, until she was right in front of Grace. "Why not?"

Grace just shook her head in silence. Tears welled in her eyes, threatening to roll down her cheeks.

"This is awful," I whispered to Marie.

"Yeah, it kind of is."

"Mrs. Chang," I started, stuttering, "Grace always wears that hat. Mrs. Suresh allows it, and I think –"

"Silence!" she snapped, glaring at me. She turned back to Grace. Taking her silence for defiance, not fear, she continued: "You're being disrespectful, holding up the entire class. Now, *please* — take the hat off."

Grace brought her eyes up to Mrs. Chang's. "I can't," she said, again. Her voice quavered.

"You *can't?* Or you *won't?*"

"I can't!"

Mrs. Chang became enraged. Her nostrils flared; her eyes grew wide. She reached forward. Grabbed the hat. Yanked.

It popped off.

For a moment, there was silence.

Then the room erupted into chaos. Screams. Vomit. Terror.

The back of Grace's head was blown open. Jagged bits of skull gave way to blood, brains, darkness. A small, matching hole sat on her forehead, near her hairline.

She'd been shot in the head.

Mrs. Chang stood in front of her — pale, frozen, terrified. Grace got up, snatched the hat back from her. For a second, she locked eyes with Mrs. Chang. As if she was going to slap her. Attack her. The classroom collectively held its breath.

Then Grace ran out of the room, sobbing.

We never saw Grace after that day. She stopped coming to school. I still don't fully understand what happened, and we don't talk about it. We're too scared to. No one can explain exactly what we saw within the walls of that history classroom.

Well, we didn't talk about it, until senior year started a few weeks ago.

There's a new kid in our class.

Who always wears a scarf.

THE CRYING WOMAN

Every night at 4 AM, without fail, I hear a woman crying in our backyard.

The first time it happened, my wife woke me up. "Harry, do you hear that?" she asked, in a terrified whisper.

Those are four words you don't want to hear in the middle of the night. Images of a home invasion raced through my mind—shots fired, our children and my pregnant wife dead in their beds. But when I strained to listen, all I heard was the sound of someone crying.

Man or woman, child or adult, I couldn't be sure.

Only one thing I knew: it was coming from right under our window.

"Is there someone out there?" Emily called from the bed.

"I don't know."

Despite the sound, when I squinted into the gray shadows, I couldn't see anyone. "I'm going to check," I said, heading for the door.

"No. Stay here, we'll call the police. Some people use recordings of babies crying to lure people out—"

I laughed. "Where'd you hear that? *Forensic Files?*" I swung the door open. "First of all, it's not a *baby*. Second of all, I won't actually go outside. I'll just take a look. I can't see jack from the window."

I went downstairs, armed with nothing more than a cell phone. But when I shined the light around through the windows, I didn't find anyone.

The crying, however, continued.

Now it sounded like it was coming from the forest surrounding our backyard. Just past the treeline. And to me, it sounded like a woman's cries; too restrained to be a child's (from experience with my kids, I know crying usually proceeds to full-out bawling in ten seconds,) and too soft and high-pitched to be a man's.

I pulled open a window, cupped my hands, and called out: "Hey! Do you need help?"

The crying sound stopped immediately.

But she didn't reply. No other sounds came from the forest, save for the wind rustling through the trees.

"Hello?" I yelled. "Anyone out there?"

A beat of silence.

Then she started screaming.

Blood-curdling shrieks. Over and over. No words, no cries for help. Just screaming.

That pushed me into action. I pulled out my phone and dialed 9-1-1. "There's a woman screaming in my backyard. I think she's hurt, or in danger. She won't respond to me. My address is XX Petunia Ave."

The stairs creaked as my wife rushed down. "Did you call the police?" I nodded. "Oh my God, what the hell is going on out there?" She kept her hand protectively over her belly, as if to shield our unborn child from whatever horrors lay outside.

My hand reached for the glass door. *What if someone is killing her? Right now? Or what if she's being abducted, and they'll both be gone by the time the police are here?*

Emily yanked me back. "No. You are not going out there."

"But—"

She pulled the door shut and locked it. "You could get killed!

Thankfully, the police arrived a minute or two later. As they walked into the backyard, the screaming cut off suddenly. Their flashlights scanned through the trees as they searched, lighting the leaves in white.

Twenty minutes later, they came back empty-handed.

They didn't find so much as a footprint in the wet mud. "Probably what you heard was the foxes," the officer said. "They've got this crazy mating call that sounds just like a woman screaming."

"But I heard her crying—"

"Look it up online," he said, with a smile. "I've been fooled by it too. They sound just like a woman screaming her lungs out. It's insane."

By the time we climbed back in bed, the gray light of dawn was spreading over the horizon. When I couldn't sleep, I took the officer's advice and looked up fox sounds. Apparently, they do make a sound that sounds pretty similar to a woman screaming.

Convincing myself that's all it was, I fell asleep.

But the next night, it happened again.

4 AM, on the dot. The soft crying, coming from the forest. I called the police again—yet again, they found nothing.

They also warned me not to call them over the crying again, unless things got worse.

And so I didn't call them when it happened the next night. And the next. And the next. I chalked it up to the foxes, even though they only made *screaming* sounds, not crying. I forced myself to fall back asleep every time.

We invested in a heavy-duty white noise machine. Bought fans, too, for good measure. Turned everything up to full blast and, for about a week, we all slept like babies. Thankfully, the kids' rooms didn't face the backyard, so they never heard a thing.

Then the night of August 24th happened.

The night started out well. Emily and I got the kids to sleep early, and we cuddled in bed for a long time— longer than we had in weeks. "Our little Ellie," I said, skimming my hand across her belly. Despite her being five months pregnant, there was barely a bump there. "Are you sure you're eating enough?"

"I'm fine," she replied, pulling my hand into hers and giving it a squeeze. "I just don't want to gain so much weight, like I did the last two times."

"You know I think you're beautiful at any weight, right?" I asked. "You don't need to do this for me."

"I'm not." She smiled, and closed her eyes. "I love you, Harry."

"I love you, too."

We fell asleep in each other's arms.

Only to be woken a few hours later by the crying.

It was louder. *Much* louder. So loud I could hear it over the white noise. As I tossed and turned my way out of a deep sleep, and pulled myself out of bed, I realized why.

It wasn't coming from the window.

It was coming from our closet.

I immediately shut off the white noise and got out of bed. "Who's there?" I yelled, my hand firmly on my phone. Ready to dial 911.

No response. Just more halting sobs, shuddering breaths, soft sniffles.

"What's going on?" Emily asked, sleepily.

"There's someone in the closet."

I turned my phone's flashlight on. The light twinkled in the darkness, bouncing off the metal doorknob. "Emily, call the police," I said, advancing towards the door.

I heard the soft sounds of the dial tone behind me — then Emily's hurried voice.

"We're calling the police," I said. "Tell me who you are!"

More sobbing.

I charged up to the door. I grasped the doorknob. With a deep breath, I twisted and pulled.

A terrified woman looked up at me.

It was Emily.

Her eyes were red and swollen. Her face was wet with a never-ending stream of tears. But it was, without a doubt, my wife. She looked exactly like the woman I'd just left in bed.

"Emily?" I whispered.

She sobbed, over and over, as she stared up at me. As if she weren't quite registering who I was.

Then I looked down, and my blood ran cold.

Her hands rested on her stomach. Her round, protruding stomach.

She was visibly pregnant.

"Harry?" Emily called from the bed. "Is everything okay?"

I looked down at the crying woman. Her sobs were silent, now—she just stared up at me, silently, tears in her eyes.

"Harry?" Emily said, more insistently this time.

I slowly shut the door. My hands were shaking; my legs were weak. When I turned around, Emily was sitting on the edge of the bed, her brown eyes locked intently at me.

"The closet was empty," I said. I walked back over to the bed, nearly fainting in the process, and sat down next to her. "I must've just imagined it."

"Aww, Harry," she said, wrapping an arm around me. I flinched at her touch. "This whole thing has been stressing you out, huh?"

I nodded.

Three knocks on the door broke through the quiet.

"Will you go let them in? I would, but I'm not dressed," she said with a light giggle, hands trailing over her silky chemise.

I didn't move from the bed.

"Harry?"

No. There was *no way* I was leaving her alone in the bedroom while I went downstairs. "I'd go down, but I don't feel so good," I lied. "I think... I just need to lie down. Will you handle it?"

She paused, staring into my eyes.

Then she finally nodded. She got off the bed, pulled on a bathrobe, and headed towards the door. As soon as she disappeared from sight, I ran to the closet.

She was still there. The woman who looked just like my wife, sitting on the floor, silently crying. The woman who *was* my wife. I don't know how I knew she was the right one—I just did. It was something intangible, a gut feeling, that I can't put into words.

I crouched down and laid my hand on her shoulders. "Emily. Emily, can you hear me?"

Her eyes stared blankly into mine. Tears streamed down her face.

"What happened to you?"

She didn't reply.

Voices murmured downstairs. Heavy footsteps resonated through the house. We were running out of time.

I grabbed her hand. "You have to come with me. Now."

She slowly, shakily, stood up. I pulled her out of the bedroom, and we softly entered the hall. Making our way to our kids' room. Downstairs, the lights were on. Emily was turned away from us, talking to the two policemen in dark outfits.

We can't let her see us.

Silence. Don't make a sound. Don't even —

Emily suddenly let go of my hand.

She ran. Her footsteps thundered across the hall as she sprinted into our kids' room. "Emily—no!" I whispered. As I ran after her, I glanced down the staircase.

Emily was staring at us. So were the police officers. Their hands were on their guns.

That's when I realized that Emily hadn't been calling 911 at all. She'd been calling for backup.

I dove into our kids' bedroom. My wife was already crouched over Abby and Mark, sobbing uncontrollably. And for the first time since I found her, she was speaking. Muttering the same three words, over and over.

"I love you."

I helped them out of bed. "Abby. Mark. We need to go. *Now."* They sleepily followed me towards the door, my wife trailing behind them.

I opened the door.

Emily stood in front of us. The two policemen stood behind her, guns raised.

"Run!" I said to Emily.

It was a risk. A huge one. They could shoot all of us in an instant. But, for some reason—they didn't. We ran down the stairs, and they chased after us. But no shots were fired.

We were alive.

As we ran out the door, I grabbed our car keys from the hook. Then we were pulling out of the driveway. The three of them stood in the doorway, watching us. Guns still raised, yet never pulling the trigger.

"Abby, Mark, are you okay?" I asked as we pulled onto the highway.

"Daddy, what's happening?" Abby asked.

"Are we in trouble?" Mark asked.

"We're okay now," I said.

We reported everything to the police, but by the time they arrived at the house, it was empty. No trace of the woman I'd called my wife for months. No trace of the two "police officers," either.

We quickly sold the house and moved several states away. Emily recovered very slowly, but she didn't seem to sustain any permanent damage. In time, she eventually told me what happened:

"It was a few months ago—about a month after we got pregnant," she said, her hands shaking as she picked up her cup of tea. "I got up to use the bathroom, and I heard someone outside. Someone crying for help. I went to the back door, opened it, and called out to see if they needed help. Then... I don't remember."

"I'm so sorry," I said, squeezing her hand.

"I kept waking up in the woods. Every time I did, I tried to make my way back to you. But all I could do was cry, and scream... it was like my mind was too foggy to form words." She squeezed my hand back. "All I could think about was you. Getting back to you, and Abby, and Mark. When I found the door unlocked one night, I walked up to our bedroom. And then—I don't remember—but I must have gotten scared, because I found myself in the closet, hiding away from your and that woman's voice. Unable to stop crying."

"I'm just glad you're back," I said, wrapping her in my arms and holding her tight.

Now, it's been almost a year since Emily and I got away. While life has been wonderful, and baby Leah is the sweetest thing... a gnawing fear has settled in my stomach. I've tried to ignore it and pass it off as stress. Anxiety. Fear. One of those haunting thoughts born out of terror, rather than logic.

But the more time that passes, the harder it is to ignore.

Our two other kids, Abby and Mark—

They haven't grown an inch since we moved here.

FLIGHT 842

Attention passengers. Flight 842 will now be departing at 7:34 PM.

My flight was delayed. Again.

I'd been sitting at gate B8 for nearly five hours. I'd drunk all my Coke, and my phone was nearly dead. I watched enviously as the stream of people walked down the terminal, towards their own gates—a woman in a bright green coat, a gaggle of giggling teenage girls—and I quietly seethed.

Their flights are on time, I bet.

They don't have to endure this hell.

I pulled myself out of the scratchy cloth chair and stormed over to the flight attendant. "It's delayed *again?!* This is the worst layover I've ever had!"

"Miss, please. We're trying as hard as we can."

"I have a wedding to get to, early tomorrow in Lancaster. I need to rent a car, check into my hotel, press my dress, and—"

I stopped.

The logo above her head did not say American Airlines. It was a strange, star-like symbol in purple, with the letters: BME.

"This... this *is* Flight 842, going to LA, right?"

"Of course," she said, with a knowing smile.

I returned to my seat. I pulled out my phone, then remembered it was nearly out of battery, and slipped it back in my pocket. Sighing, I leaned back and stared out at the people going by.

A man with a handlebar mustache. A tired mother in yoga pants dragging two little boys by the hand. A man in a crisp business suit, talking into one of those fancy earpieces.

And, after him—

The same woman in the bright-green coat.

Wait, what? That's weird. I never saw her pass by in the other direction. But, then again... I was occupied talking to the flight attendant.

Nothing to worry about. I reached in my bag, found the crushed chocolate bar I'd tucked away, and began to pick at it. Flakes of chocolate crumbled onto my lap, and I sighed.

I glanced up—

To see a familiar man with a handlebar mustache.

I watched in horror as he was followed by the tired mother, pulling her little boys by the arms. The businessman, talking into his earpiece.

They're walking in a loop. But the hallway didn't seem to curve at all.

What is going on?

My heart began to pound. I leapt out of my seat and walked towards them, without even knowing what I was going to say. "Uh, excuse me!" I called out to the mom.

She didn't turn around.

"Excuse me! Hey!"

They ignored me, like I wasn't even there. Not even a single glance from the boys. I opened my mouth to shout again, but then the voice came over the intercom:

"We are now boarding Flight 842. Please get in the queue."

I glanced back. The other people at the gate were slowly getting up, gravitating towards the line. As they did, I realized—

They had no luggage.

No suitcases. No backpacks. Not even purses.

No luggage at all.

They mechanically moved forward in the line, holding out their boarding passes. *Beep! Beep!* The flight attendant scanned each one, and they disappeared into the aluminum tunnel.

My gaze flicked to the window.

It was dark out. Too dark. How had I not noticed that before? There were no blinking lights from the runway. No lights coming off the plane. No moon, no stars, no lights from the city around us.

Just darkness.

"Are you coming?"

I jumped. The flight attendant was standing right behind me, her lips curled into that knowing smile.

Every single person in the line, too, had snapped towards me. They watched intently, scowling, glaring.

I backed away. "No. No, I'm not—"

She grabbed my wrist. "You can't back out now."

I wrenched my arm free from her grip and ran, abandoning my luggage. I darted out of the gate, into the main aisle. Then I ran, and ran, until my legs ached and I could barely breathe.

"Ma'am? Are you alright?"

I looked up to see a security guard standing in front of me. "I... I was at B8 and this woman... she tried to make me board and—"

"B8?"

"Yeah."

"Ma'am, we don't have any B8 gate."

"What? My flight said B8," I said, pulling out the crinkled boarding pass. I shoved it into his hands.

"No, that's B6."

I glanced at my boarding pass again. The 6... I'd mistaken it for an 8. "I'm sorry," I mumbled, walking away.

I walked back down the hall. He was right—the gates skipped from B7 to B9. A stretch of white wall spanned between them.

No waiting room. No gate.

Just wall.

THE HALLOWEEN MASK
by Blair Daniels & Craig Groshek

Ding!

I jolted awake.

My phone lit up on the nightstand. It showed one new notification: *Motion detected at your doorstep. 3:17 AM.*

My heart pounded as my fingers slipped across the screen. I clicked on the security camera video feed.

A man stood on my doorstep.

He stayed so still, I would've thought it was a photograph, if not for the bugs fluttering by every few seconds. His body melted into the shadows around him, but his face shone brightly. Or—not his face. A white mask.

It was covered in blood.

He stared straight at the camera, completely still, mouth twisted in a grin.

***

It all started when I ordered the Halloween mask.

Alicia and I decided to host the neighborhood Halloween party this year. I'd shelled out hundreds of dollars on plastic skulls, purple streamers, and even one of those candy bowls with the animatronic hand in the middle.

"We still need to decide what to dress up as," my wife said, as she neatly stacked the boxes in the corner. "I was thinking maybe Morticia and Gomez—"

"No. That's cliché."

Alicia rolled her eyes. "So *what* if it's cliché? It's just a neighborhood party."

"It has to be perfect."

"Well, whatever it is, you better decide soon. The party's next weekend."

I scrolled through costumes online, looking for something terrifying. Something our neighbors would remember for years to come. Last year, the party was hosted by my rival neighbor, David Chandler. Ugh. Perfectly handsome, BMW-driving David. My very own Ned Flanders, one-upping me on everything from lawn care to job promotions.

Last year he threw an incredible party, dressed as the clown from *It*. He even jump-scared half the guests at various points throughout the evening. People were *still* talking about how awesome it was.

I had to do better.

"What about that?" Alicia asked, pointing to a plain white mask.

It looked similar to a Michael Myers mask. White plastic, forming the shape of a man's face, with cut-outs for the eyes and the mouth. "You could make it your own. Add blood, or stitches, or something."

"True." I clicked it, and Google took me to some costume website I'd never heard of before. I added it to my cart, and after scouring the web for some promo codes—I didn't have much money left after all I'd spent on decorations—found a sketchy-looking website with what *appeared* to be a legitimate promo URL displayed, with the offer code worked into it. Without thinking, I clicked it.

As soon as I did so, I was redirected somewhere that was *definitely* not the website displayed in the URL. *Damn it*, I thought, *I should have copied and pasted the link instead of clicking it directly.* As I pondered how many viruses I'd just been infected with, and before I could do anything else, a strange message popped up, taking up my entire screen.

CODE INPUT SUCCESSFULLY
SELECT YOUR SCARE

1. #$@
2. &+?
3. *&#

"What the hell is this?" I muttered. I tried to just click away from the dialog box, but it wouldn't disappear. Finally, against my better judgment I clicked the first option, just to make it go away. I was happy to see I was back on the website I'd originally intended to order from, with my item still in my shopping cart, and the promo code successfully applied. *I can't believe it,* I thought. *It actually worked.*

With that important Halloween-related task checked off my list, but many things left to take care of, I went on with my day, and quickly forgot all about the strange pop-up, and eagerly awaited my new mask.

***

A few days later, I got an email telling me the package had arrived—October 29, two days before the party. But when I got home, I found an empty doorstep.

"You didn't see a package?" I asked Alicia.

"Didn't you get the notification?" she asked, pinning up purple and orange streamers. "We were the victim of a *porch pirate.*" She pulled out her phone and handed it to me. "Check it out."

We have one of those security cameras by the door—mostly to avoid Bob, our resident traveling salesman, who seems to be selling something new every week. Whenever motion is detected, it pings our phones; today I'd been swamped at work, though, and hadn't had a chance to look at it.

I pressed play.

I saw our doorstep—and the brown cardboard box sitting on the doorstep. Behind it, on the sidewalk, was a figure in black.

I watched as the man approached. He walked up my sidewalk with confidence, as if he lived here. As soon as he got close—close enough for me to see his face—he tilted his pale head down.

Then he stepped onto my porch, and, face still hidden, grabbed the package.

He walked back down the sidewalk and disappeared.

"Why would he steal a package of Halloween costumes?"

"Because your costume was just *so amazing,* he wanted it for himself," Alicia joked, as she lined up bags of candy.

"It wasn't amazing yet. It's just the mask." I walked over to the table and helped her set up the candy. "So we have two days, right? What else needs to be done?"

"Well, we need to get new costumes, and I was thinking—"

"Morticia and Gomez?" I sighed. "Fine. We'll do it."

I thought that would be the end of it—some guy stole the package, and that was it. We'd never see the mask again.

I was sorely mistaken.

As I sat at the table a few hours later, dumping candy into decorative bowls, a flash of motion caught my eye. I looked up—and saw someone walking in our backyard. At the edge of the woods.

They were dressed entirely in black, walking along the perimeter of the forest. In the dusk light, it was hard to pick out any details about them—like their gender, or their face. The only thing I could see was that they walked with slow, deliberate movements.

And it looked like they were wearing a white mask.

I heard Alicia's footsteps behind me and motioned her over. "Alicia, look. There's someone in our backyard."

"What? Seriously?"

She joined me at the window. But by the time she did, the person had already disappeared into the forest.

"I'm going up to bed," Alicia said. "We can finish this tomorrow."

I followed her up. Minutes after my head hit the pillow, I fell into a deep sleep.

Until I woke up an hour later.

I looked at the clock. 1:34 AM. I pulled myself out of bed and trudged over to the bathroom, eyes blurred with sleep.

The moonlight shone in from the window. I walked over to it, as if drawn by the light, and peered into the backyard below.

I froze.

At the edge of the backyard was a figure.

Dressed in all black. Wearing a white mask. Facing our house, standing still as a statue.

My heart pounded. I reached for my phone—then remembered it was still on the nightstand. I raced over and grabbed it, then looked back out the window.

He was gone.

***

The next day, in the flurry of getting ready for the party, I forgot about what I'd seen the night before. Around 6 PM, I headed out to the party store to pick up some last-minute things.

There I received a text from Alicia.

That was odd, in of itself. I knew she had an important call with a client that evening. Confused, I opened the text.

What it said made no sense.

I'm glad you found your mask, but can you please stop? I'm on the phone with Evelyn.

I quickly texted back:

Stop what?

She replied:

Stop tapping on the window! It's super annoying.

I stared at my phone, panic seeping in. Then my fingers raced across the keyboard, as I typed:

I'm not at home. I'm at the party store.

She didn't reply. I grabbed my stuff and ran out to the car, phone pressed against my ear.

I breathed a sigh of relief when she answered.

"Ben? I told you, I'm on the phone—"

"Alicia, I'm not home. Whoever you're seeing out there *isn't me.* You need to call the police, right now." Memories of the figure I'd seen the night before rushed back to me, and I shuddered.

"But—"

"Call the police!" I yelled.

When I arrived home, the police were already there. Red and blue lights, flashing in the darkness of our driveway. Alicia stood in the driveway, giving her statement, somewhat begrudgingly. "All I saw was someone in a black hoodie, black pants, and a white mask with fake blood all over it. They were over there, at the office window."

"You didn't recognize anything about them?" the tall, lanky officer asked.

"I thought it was my husband, but he was at the store, apparently. Look—I'm sure it's just some teenager from the neighborhood playing a mischief night prank. And if it is," she said, giving me a stern look as I walked over, "I don't want to press charges. We were all young and dumb once."

The officer laughed at that. An annoying, high-pitched laugh that grated my eardrums. "We'll take a look around and follow up with you, Mrs. Breslaw," he said.

"Thank you."

Alicia turned to me—arms crossed, lips pressed into a line. "Great. You just wasted twenty minutes of my time. Evelyn is so pissed that I cut the call short."

"There was some creep tapping on your window!" I shouted back. "What, you wanted to just ignore it?"

"Obviously just some teenager. I mean, come on, it's mischief night. I'm just happy it was that and not getting TP'd. That takes forever to clean up."

"Okay. Fine." I hurried past her and set my supplies on the table. Then I set to work ripping open packs of plastic spiders and bats. They fell onto the table with loud, gross *plops*.

"I'm going upstairs," Alicia said curtly, leaving me to prepare for the party on my own.

***

Ding!
Motion detected at your doorstep. 3:17 AM.
The notification came through on my phone, loud and clear. I tapped on the video feed, half-asleep.

A man stood on my doorstep.

He wore all black. Covering his face was the white mask I'd ordered, covered in something dark.

I jumped out of bed. "Alicia," I whispered, shaking her awake. "Alicia. He's back."

"What?" she murmured.

"The man in the mask. He's back. He's standing on our porch right now and—"

"Is he TP'ing the trees?"

"No."

"Then let me sleep," she groaned, rolling over and throwing the covers over her head.

I know lots of crazy things happen on mischief night. But this crossed a line. A big line. A man standing on my porch in the middle of the night, wearing the mask I'd ordered? Probably the same man who'd stolen the mask in the first place, right off my doorstep?

This was too far.

I crept out of the room and peered down into the foyer. Through the glass insert in our door, I saw him.

He stood under the porch light, blurred and distorted through the glass, but I could still make out the white mask. Stained red with blood.

Should I call the police?

Alicia would be mad at me. But screw it. This was too far.

My fingers slipped over the screen. "There's a man standing on my porch, in a mask," I said, my words coming out as a jumbled string of syllables.

As soon as the call ended, the figure shifted. Then it receded, until all that remained was the empty porch. I clicked back to the security camera feed; it, too, showed nothing but the empty porch and the shadows of the front yard.

A sharp knock on the door tore me from my thoughts. I looked down to see two figures distorted through the glass: two figures wearing blue uniforms.

I let the police in and explained everything. I even showed them the security footage. They scoured the backyard—but they didn't find anyone.

When they finally left, I retreated back into the bedroom. Alicia, thankfully, somehow slept through it all.

I locked the door and dragged a dresser over it for good measure. Then I collapsed into the bed. I didn't fall asleep until the sky brightened with dawn and the birds began to sing.

***

"Aren't you excited for the party?"

I stared out the window like a soulless zombie. I'd slept all of three hours, and the fatigue felt like a train driving over me, again and again.

But I couldn't nap—there was so much to do. Spider cupcakes and monster fingers to bake. Decorations to hang. Candy bowls to put out.

"Will you hang these streamers in the office?" Alicia asked, handing me a tangled mess of black, orange, and purple.

"But no one will be going in there."

She quirked an eyebrow at me. "You told me you wanted this to be the best party ever. That you wanted every single room decorated, just in case."

"Okay, okay," I said, forcing myself out of the chair. I took the streamers from her and entered the office.

There, on the desk, was the mask.

Mouth twisted into a smile. Gaping holes for eyes. Dark red splattered across the plastic.

"Alicia!" I shouted.

She rushed into the room. "Where... where'd you get this mask?" I stuttered, breathless.

"It was on our doorstep this morning."

Relief flooded through me. *He wasn't in the house. It was just on the doorstep.* My entire body shook as I fell into the chair.

"Why don't you rest for a bit before the party starts?" Alicia said, laying a hand on my shoulder. "I'll call you down when everyone's here."

I nodded.

Alicia thought I was overreacting. Maybe she was right; maybe I was letting a mischief night prank by some dumb teenager mess with my head. I lay down on the bed, ignoring the *dings* of my phone on the nightstand, and closed my eyes.

It seemed like only seconds passed before Alicia was back in the room, asking me to come downstairs. "Everyone's here," she said. "And they want to see you." I followed her down the stairs.

And froze.

Every single person in the room wore the mask.

Black clothes with that white mask over their faces, covered in splatters of blood. Gaping eye holes, a twisted mouth.

I felt dizzy. The room pitched before me, and I gripped the banister for balance.

"Ben? Are you okay?"

I swayed, trying to steady myself. "Why... why are they all wearing that?"

"They said you asked them to."

"What?"

"You didn't?"

"No," I said, as the crowd blurred before me.

"They said you left the masks with a note, saying they should wear them to the party. A lot of people canceled because of it. Families with kids, mostly." She turned to me. "You really didn't do it?"

"Why would I?!"

Alicia shrugged. "I don't know. You were obsessed with this party from the beginning. And the mask. I thought maybe..." She trailed off. "If you didn't put the masks in their mailboxes, who did?"

Him. The man who had been tapping on the window. The man who had been standing on our porch last night.

The man who stole my mask.

As my mind swirled with questions—who he was, why he'd do this—a memory popped into my head. The promo code, and the "SELECT YOUR SCARE" message.

Had I somehow chosen this?

I stared into the crowd. Fifty masked faces stared back at me. All identical. Anyone could be him. Or no one.

Before I could think, a hand pulled me into the crowd.

"Ben, hey! How's it going?" a familiar voice asked behind the mask. Eddie Huntley, the blond-haired man that lived three houses down the street.

"It's good," I said, faking a smile.

He continued to talk, but I only pretended I was listening. I looked across the crowd. All the masked faces were turned towards each other, bobbing and nodding in conversation.

Except for one.

Who was staring right at me.

I broke away from the conversation. "Hey—*hey!*" I shouted, pushing through the crowd. His gaping eyes stared back at mine. Soulless. Empty.

I grabbed the mask and ripped it off.

And stared into the face of Marie Chandler. The wife of my rich, luxury-loving neighbor. "Ben! Great party. Love the masks," she said in her elegant, soft voice. "Really adds a creepy flavor to the whole thing."

"Th-thanks," I stuttered.

"Hey, have you seen David? It seems I've lost him."

I shook my head.

She continued staring into the crowd.

Ding. My phone chimed. I slowly pulled it out of my pocket and looked at the screen. *Motion detected at your doorstep. 8:32 PM.*

I tapped on the camera feed.

There he stood.

David?

Who else could it be? He was missing, and there was the masked man, standing on my porch. Heart pounding, I fought my way through the kitchen, through the family room, and over to the front door.

Now the porch was empty.

I opened the door and stared out into the night. But beyond the halo of light the porch created, everything was a murky mess of shadow. I shut the door.

The lights flickered.

And then they went out.

The room plunged into darkness. Shouts and murmurs sounded across the party. Masked faces whirled about in confusion. "Turn the lights back on!" a woman shouted angrily. Cell phone flashlights flicked on, twinkling among the crowd of shadows.

Ding.

Motion detected at your backdoor. 8:35 PM.

I stared at my phone in horror as I heard the back door creak open. Followed by heavy footsteps. I ran through the family room, and into the kitchen.

The back door hung open, but he was gone.

Blended into the crowd.

Stay calm, I told myself. *Get the power back on. Then you can deal with finding the culprit.* My head pulsed with pain as I considered the two options. Either someone flipped the master breaker... or someone cut the power lines.

I decided to check the master breaker first.

"Alicia," I said, fumbling my way in the darkness towards her. Thank goodness she wasn't wearing a mask like the rest of them. "Keep everyone calm, okay? I'm going to check the breakers in the basement."

"Okay," she said, biting her lip. "You think maybe the fog machine was drawing too much power?"

"Uh... yeah."

No need to get her worried.

Using my cell phone as a flashlight, I stumbled to the basement door. I opened it. The stairs loomed before me, stretching into the pitch black below. A shudder ran through me. "Maybe it was just the fog machine," I muttered to myself, descending the steps one-by-one. We had a menagerie of Halloween decorations out on the lawn, and it was possible that they blew a fuse.

Then why would the whole house be without power?

I forced the question out of my head and continued down the stairs. I made my way to the breaker box, my footsteps clicking against the cement.

The master breaker was flipped.

Someone intentionally walked into the basement and flipped the switch. My heart pounded in my chest; my hand shook as I reached out and flipped the switch back. The lights flickered to life, including the lightbulb above my head.

For a second, silence.

Then someone grabbed me roughly from behind.

I whipped around, thrashing against strong arms. A white mask stared back at me, smeared with blood. Gaping, empty eye sockets.

I tore away and jumped back. My body collided with my workbench. My eyes scanned it—there was my hammer, lying on the wood.

I grabbed it.

The figure jumped forward. Laughter echoed from beneath the mask, along with a voice. "I got you this ti—"

I lifted the hammer.

And smashed it into his skull.

The man immediately crumpled. He fell onto the floor, head smacking against the tile. I crouched over him. Then I reached over and pulled the mask off.

It was David.

Footsteps sounded behind me. Then shouts, then screams. "Call 911!" someone cried.

But David was perfectly still.

***

The police carried him out in a body bag.

The guests were gone. The masks were strewn across the floor, the couch, every room of the house. A few were completely crushed, stepped on in the chaos. The back door still hung open, letting in gusts of cold October air.

I didn't sleep a wink that night. The image of David's face burned into my mind. I'd heard his wife explain to the police, in broken sobs, that he'd been planning some sort of prank on me at the party. He hadn't visited the house, or stalked Alicia; he'd only planned a scare at the party. She didn't know what it was until the lights went out.

He was innocent.

I spent half the day sleeping, the other half drunk. When night rolled around, Alicia pulled me off the couch. "Sit out on the porch with me," she said.

"Why?"

"It isn't good for you to be inside all day, like this."

I followed her out, beer in hand. We sat on the back porch, facing the forest. "Ben, you can't... you didn't mean to," she forced out, glancing in my direction.

"No. I didn't mean to."

"The funeral's in three days. Maybe we should go." She reached out and squeezed my hand.

"I don't know if I can face Marie," I said, stumbling over my words. "Or any of them. I—"

My words caught in my throat.

There, on the edge of the treeline, stood a familiar figure. Dressed in all black. Wearing a white mask splattered with blood.

I stood up. Alicia grabbed my hand, but I yanked it away. "Get the hell off my property!" I screamed.

The figure didn't budge.

Fueled by alcohol and anger, I leapt off the porch and strode across the backyard. "Ben—please don't—" Alicia called after me.

"Take off your fucking mask!" I screamed, closing in on the figure. He still didn't move. "A man is dead because of you and your fucking games!"

Alicia jogged after me, turning on her cell's flashlight. "Ben, please, stop!"

But I didn't stop. I didn't stop until I was inches from his face, until I could smell his sordid breath in the air. "Take off your fucking mask," I growled. "I want to see who you are, before I smash your stupid little head."

He just stared at me with those gaping eye sockets, plastic mouth twisted into a smile.

"Oh, you don't believe me? You should. I killed someone last night. Smashed his head right in. I'm a murderer now. You hear that?" I leaned in, my face inches from his. "I killed someone because of you! And I'll kill you, too, if you don't take that fucking mask off!"

He didn't move.

"Fine!" I shouted, spittle flying from my mouth. "I'll take it off myself, then."

I reached up. Grabbed at his jawline. Pulled.

It didn't come off.

I stumbled forward. Grabbed harder. Pulled harder.

"No. No, no, no..." I took a step back, my heart pounding.

It wasn't a mask.

I watched in horror as his mirthful grin contorted into an angry scowl. "Run!" I screamed, taking off across the grass. Alicia followed, screaming her lungs out. I whipped around to see the figure chasing us full speed across the lawn.

I ran as fast as I could. I didn't stop until I was inside the house, closing the door.

That's when I realized.

Alicia had stopped screaming. The backyard was empty—both of them were gone without a trace.

Except for Alicia's phone in the grass. The flashlight shined up towards the sky, shimmering and sparkling in the shadows.

***

I haven't seen Alicia since that night.

It's been a week. I didn't attend David's funeral, though I suppose I am now in the same boat as Marie Chandler. Her husband is gone; so is my wife.

The police suspect that I killed David on purpose. After all, our playful little rivalry was well-known among neighbors. They also believe I had something to do with Alicia's disappearance, and to fill in a motive for me, rumors are flying that Alicia and David were having an affair.

I've been advised not to leave town. So, as much as I would love to leave this all behind, I'm stuck here. With my guilt. With the past.

I leave you with a warning. The masked man— whatever he is—is still out there. And so, I beg you: don't trust anyone who wears a mask. Who hides their face behind a grotesque facade of plastic.

Because it might not be a mask, after all.

FACEAPP

"FaceApp" is an app that shows you what you'll look like old. This afternoon, I downloaded it, after a healthy dose of peer pressure.

"Come on. I want to see what you look like," my husband said, a grin on his face.

Sure he did. He still looked handsome, with the spattering of silver hair and distinguished lines on his face. Me? I'd probably look like an old hag.

The app loaded. I took a photo and scrolled through the options. I tapped "Age." Then "Old."

The spinning icon showed up as it loaded. I held my breath.

The image appeared.

I froze.

It didn't show me with gray hair, or wrinkles, or yellow teeth. No — it was so much worse.

My skin stretched over my cheekbones, thin and papery, a sickly shade of gray. My eyes were clouded white, the pupils barely visible. My dark brown hair had no gray — but it was tangled and knotted around my face. Half my teeth were gone.

I didn't look old.

I looked *dead.*

"What? What's wrong?" Alex asked.

I quickly slid the phone out of his view. "It's nothing. Just... don't want you to see me like this."

That part was true.

"Fiiiine." He pulled away and have me a smile. "I'll just have to wait until you get old, then." He winked at me.

I gave him an awkward smile back.

"I should get back to work," he said, heading towards our home office. "But we'll go out to dinner tonight, okay?"

I nodded.

As soon as he'd left the room, I pulled the phone out again. Stared at the photo.

It looked even worse than I remembered. As I brought it close to my face, I noticed a worm making its way through my hair. It had been nearly camouflaged against my brown hair. And my skin was mottled not with age spots, but actual holes.

Then I realized.

I can't be the only one.

I pulled up a new tab and started searching. After wading through the various news articles on the app, I found a forum with a few users talking about it.

Hey. When I did the FaceApp aging thing, instead of seeing an old person, I saw myself... like rotted and dead, and stuff. Did that happen to anyone else?

A few replies indicated it had.

Yeah, I look like some zombie, LOL

I think it's a glitch. This is new software and they're still ironing everything out.

I think they put it in there as a prank.

I breathed a sigh of relief. But then, just as I was getting comfortable, my eyes fell on a fourth reply:

I think there's something more to it. I don't want to scare you, but... my sister got the exact thing you described. Showed her all dead, like a zombie.

She has terminal brain cancer.

My heart stopped. I felt hot. Itchy. Dizzy. I stood up and swept a hand over my face, as if I expected to find the holes. The worm. Everything.

I raced up, ran into the bathroom. Splashed water on my skin. The face looking back at me looked no different than it did yesterday. Or the day before.

But the horrifying words now pulsed through my head.

It didn't show me old...

Because I'm not going to make it to old age.

BLIND SPOT

"It's the best car on the lot."

The salesman gestured to the SUV in front of us. It was beautiful: sleek curves, iridescent red paint. All the edges and corners smoothed, lending resemblance to a bullet train.

"It's a fantastic deal. A good five thousand below market price. It's even got all the safety features," Mr. Craggs said, as his hand trailed along the car's hood. "Lane departure, blind spot detection..."

"But it's used, right?" my husband asked.

"Yes, it's *pre-owned,*" the salesman corrected. "Previous owner only had it a few weeks, though."

My husband liked everything brand new. Out-of-the-box, untouched by man. He paced around the car, sipping his third cup of free coffee, a frown on his face. Then his eyes met Mr. Craggs's. "If it's such a great car, why did they get rid of it?"

Mr. Craggs's face fell. He began to stutter. "They, uh... passed away. It was a lease, so the car reverted back to us."

A thick silence fell over the three of us. I uncomfortably glanced from Luke to Mr. Craggs. "Was it something contagious? Like a disease, or —"

Mr. Craggs shook his head, waved his hand dismissively. "No, nothing like that. I think it was a heart attack." The fake smile finally reformed on his face. "Would you like to see the inside?"

I opened the door, climbed in... and fell in love. The leather-wrapped steering wheel. The ergonomic seat. The buttons and dials, shiny and black. When Luke stepped in, he scrunched his nose.

"Smells terrible."

I sniffed. It did smell off – rotten and putrid, mixed with the an acrid, chemical burn. As if someone had vomited, left it to sit for a few days, then cleaned it up with bleach. I knew that smell all too well, from my days as designated driver. But I shot Luke a smile and said innocently, "I don't smell anything."

"You don't smell that? Really?"

I shook my head.

"I think we should just pick something else. Something new."

"Are you kidding?" I pulled out my phone. "Look. He's not lying – market value for a car like this is twenty-five thousand. This is the deal of the century."

"It's someone else's junk."

Anger bubbled in my chest. I wanted to tell him everything – that I thought he was being picky. Spoiled. Unfair. Instead, I took a deep breath, and replied: "I know we're not used to buying used cars. But now, we're going to have to."

A few weeks ago, Luke had been laid off from Beagle & O'Marr, Attorneys at Law. He got a new job at some dinky little firm in rural Michigan; I found work online. We packed up our bags and moved out of the city — trading skyscrapers for sprawling forest, concert halls for coffee shops, movie stars for starry skies.

"We could get a new sedan, instead," he said. "That'd be the same price."

"And how do you think we'll survive the winter?"

In the city, the roads were plowed with alacrity. Not so out here, in the middle of East Jabib. It was only November, and we'd already gotten snowed in twice.

"Fine. We'll do it." He gulped down the last dregs of coffee, wincing at the taste.

It took us ten minutes to sign the papers. Then we were sitting in the car – *our* car – feeling the seats warm under us. The engine hummed softly; the stereo cut through the air, crisp and clear. It rode like a dream — dipping smoothly over the potholes, over the cracked asphalt.

As we neared the house, we got our first taste of the safety features.

Beep, beep, beep.

"That's the blind spot detection! See the little orange light, on my mirror? Someone's passing us."

"They got some nerve," Luke replied, gripping the steering wheel. "I'm going forty-five. And these lanes are awfully narrow."

We waited for the car to pass.

It never came.

Confused, I glanced back. The road was empty. Not a single pair of headlights, even in the distance. Just the dark, country road, snaking back into the shadows of the pines.

"There's no one there. It must be broken."

Luke snickered under his breath. "That's what you get for buying a used car."

The anger flared again, but I held my tongue. When we got home, I stole inside without a word. When I opened the door, the smell hit me like a wave: garbage, must, firewood. And it was so cold. The chill breezed through the door, crept in through cracks in the wall.

"It's cold in here," Luke said, reaching for the thermostat.

I turned around and shot him a glare. "We're trying to keep the electricity bill down, remember? Suck it up and grab a sweater."

Unlike Luke, I was used to this. I grew up in a manufactured home on the outskirts of Detroit, with barely enough food to feed the five of us. The heat was often shut off entirely, dipping the temperature into the 40s.

He pulled a fleece over his head and sat down beside me. "Is it always going to be like this?" His tone wasn't angry. It was desperate.

I reached out and squeezed his hand. "No," I said. "It won't."

I hoped that was the truth.

***

"What do we have for dinner? Any chicken left?"

The nightly conversation about dinner. It almost always ended in a fight, as Luke would propose eating out, I'd suggest eating in, and we'd both argue about it for an hour. Growing hungrier, and in turn, angrier. A vicious cycle.

"No, just the tomato soup," I said, for the second time that evening.

"That's not enough. I'm starving."

"Well, that's all we got."

"Then let's go out someplace." He must've seen the scowl on my face, because he quickly followed up with: "it doesn't have to be expensive. We can just do fast food."

"Okay. Fine."

We walked out the back door. The sun had already slipped beneath the tall, black pines, and the temperature was quickly dropping. Pink and gold streaked across the sky, as if applied by a paintbrush. Deep, blue shadows crept along the brown grass, the leftover bits of snow.

I turned the corner — and stopped dead in my tracks.

The car's headlights were on.

"You left the headlights on?" I snapped, turning to Luke. "That'll run the battery down! Then we'll have to get someone out here, and –"

"I didn't leave them on," he replied.

"Oh, come on."

"I didn't, Katy."

I stepped towards the car. Luke stretched his hand out in front of me. "Wait. Let me go first." He took a step forward. "Hello?" he called, approaching the car.

No reply.

"You think someone's there?" I whispered to him.

"No. It's just... I'm *sure* I turned those headlights off."

We crept closer to the car. In the blinding light, I could barely make out the car, let alone the inside. For all I knew, someone *was* sitting in the car. Waiting for us.

Luke walked over to the driver's side door. The lights flicked off; he gave me a thumbs-up.

We climbed inside. "Maybe the car is haunted," I joked, pulling the seatbelt across my lap.

He laughed as the engine sputtered to life. "Oh, right. I forgot about that."

"Do you think he died here? Right in the car?"

"It's possible. That would certainly explain the smell. He died in here, but they didn't find his body for a week —"

"Ew! Luke!" I smacked him across the arm. "Don't tell me that!"

He snickered.

We drove in silence for a few minutes, watching the sun sink below the horizon. A few flakes of snow danced in the headlights; I smiled, knowing we were safe in our four-wheel drive.

We picked up speed on Highland Avenue. That's when the blind spot detector went off.

Beep, beep, beep.

The orange light flashed in my sideview mirror. I glanced back – but, just like yesterday, the road was empty behind us. Stretching back into the forest, cutting pines like a ribbon of smoke.

"Someone passing us?" Luke asked.

"Nope." I sighed. "Maybe you're right. Haunted or not, this thing is a piece of junk."

"It's not that bad." He shot me a smile. "Doesn't even smell much anymore. Or, maybe, I've just gotten used to it."

"Yeah, I think it still —"

My breath caught in my throat.

There was a car behind us.

It wasn't there a second ago. But there it was, now — a sleek, black sedan, hovering right in the passenger-side blind spot. Despite the gathering darkness, its headlights were off. When the streetlamps fell away, it melted into the shadows.

I couldn't see it in my sideview mirror. Or the rearview. It was invisible in every single mirror—but when I turned around, there it was.

"There's someone trying to pass us."

"I thought you said —"

"I must've missed it the first time."

"Alright, I'll let them go." Luke applied the brakes. We slowed.

Almost immediately, the black car slowed, too. Like it was *trying* to stay exactly in our blind spot.

"It's not passing us."

"Roll down your window, then, and wave them on."

I rolled down the window. The icy air gust into the car, slapping at my face. Cringing, I waved it on.

It didn't budge.

The car just hovered there, right in our blind spot. Matching our speed perfectly. That's when I noticed something was wrong with it.

The windshield was tinted glass, completely obscuring the driver inside. All I could see were the reflections of the sunset, the pines, the clouds scrolling across the glass.

"They've got a tinted windshield. Isn't that against the law?"

"I think so."

My mind reeled with the possibilities. *What if they're drug dealer? A getaway car?* There was no *good* reason to have tinted glass, to hide from the world.

Beep, beep, beep. The blind spot detector went off again. A warning.

"I don't like this. It makes me nervous, how they're just following us like that."

"Yeah. Agreed. Let's see if we can get them to pass." Luke hit the brakes again. This time, we slowed to a crawl. Route 207 had a speed limit of 45 miles per hour; we were now going 20.

The seconds ticked by. *1, 2, 3...*

Whrrrrrm.

The car whizzed past us. I let out a sigh of relief and watched it fade into the darkness. "That was so weird," I said, leaning back in my seat.

"Bet they're high, or something."

"Do you think we should report it?"

"Did you get a look at the license plate?"

"No."

"Then, there's not much we can do."

The engine roared under our feet as we reached the speed limit again, and we fell into silence. I watched the pines scroll past the window, the hills of snow rise and fall with each second. The fire of sunset had now faded, replaced with deep hues of purple. My cheek fell against the cool glass; my body relaxed against the seat. My eyes fluttered closed.

Beep, beep, beep.

I jolted up.

It was back. Hovering right in my blind spot. Closer now — just a foot or two from our car. Headlights off, barely more than a silhouette.

"It's back," I said, my voice quavering.

"What — the car?" Luke glanced over his shoulder. "No. There's no way it could've passed us, turned around, and caught up with us again."

"It has to be. It looks the same. Tinted windows. Headlights off." My heart pounded; fear thrummed through me. I glanced ahead of us, then behind.

We were the only two cars on the road.

"Okay. If that's how he wants to play this, fine." Luke's brows furrowed, and he pursed his lips. "Hold tight."

The engine hummed, then roared.

We shot forward. The highway flit by beneath us. The intermittent streetlamps flashed across our car faster and faster, like strobe lights. The pines smudged into lines of black and gray against the purple sky.

I glanced at the speedometer. *Eighty-five, ninety...*

A roar pierced the silence behind us. I turned around. The car was gaining fast. Like a panther chasing its prey.

"Luke, stop!"

The car was upon us, now. Hovering in our blind spot. Then, with a screech of tires, the gap between their hood and my door started to close.

They were swerving right into us.

"No!" I reached over and grabbed the steering wheel from Luke. I yanked it left. The car swerved madly underneath us.

Beep, beep, beep.

"It's still there. Oh, God, it's still —"

I turned back. I could see the silhouette of a person, vaguely outlined in the darkness, underneath the tinted glass. Whether male or female, young or old, I couldn't tell.

I screamed as the gap closed.

Crunch.

My door crumpled on impact. My body tossed wildly to the left, like a rag doll.

"Katy!" Luke jerked at the steering wheel; the car swerved.

It was too late.

Crack!

Metal punched metal. This time, the door caved in. Cold winter air swept in. The car reeled against the black road. The world whipped together outside — forest with road, sky with snow, all sucked into a vortex of color and shadow.

I heard Luke call my name.

Then there was only darkness.

***

My eyes fluttered open.

Our car stood in the center of the empty road. The passenger side was destroyed—the buckled door cut my space in half, and the window was shattered, scattering bits of safety glass everywhere. Skidding tire tracks spiraled around the car.

I glanced over to the driver's side. Luke was slumped against the wheel. "Luke! Luke, are you okay?!"

"I think I am," he groaned, slowly pulling himself up.

"We need to call the police." I bent over and groped for my phone on the floor. My hands only hit shards of glass. "Dammit! Do you have your phone?"

"No—I don't think so." He felt his pockets.

"Shit," I whispered, hands brushing across the carpet. "Where the hell is it?! It's got to be here somewh—"

Beep, beep, beep.

The orange light flashed.

I slowly turned around. Behind me, lurking in the shadows, was the black car. Headlights off, it crawled forward. "He's... he's behind us," I whispered.

Luke twisted the key. The engine sputtered, then quickly died away. The black car stopped a few feet behind us.

Then the door opened.

I watched in horror as a male figure stepped out. A black shadow, advancing towards us in the sideview mirror. I clicked the locks. As if that would help — my entire window was gone.

Click, click, click.

His footsteps sounded on the damp pavement.

"Luke! He's coming towards us!" I shouted. Luke turned the ignition, tried to start the car again. It sputtered again.

I turned my head away from the window. I couldn't look. Couldn't watch. But a few seconds later, the cold wind that swept across my neck suddenly died away. A shadow fell over my face. Warm air fell against my ear, acrid and rotten.

He was standing right outside my window.

"No, no, no," I sobbed, under my breath. "Please, no —"

Rrrrrmm.

The roar of an engine cut through the air.

We lurched forward. Luke stared straight ahead as he mashed down on the pedal. Our car shot through the darkness, the right headlight flickering madly.

Beep, beep, beep.

The left sideview mirror lit up.

"Shut up!" Luke screamed at it. "Shut up, shut up!"

Neither of us turned around. We knew what was hovering in our blind spot, ready to crash into us at any moment.

An sign flashed in our headlights. CULLEN ROAD. "Pull off!" I shouted.

He jerked the wheel. The car swerved off the road at the last second. We shot through the turn, and found ourselves in a small town. I whipped around. There was no sign of the black car.

"I see a sign for a hospital," Luke said. "Don't know what else is around here."

We made a few turns, and then we were in the hospital parking lot.

We climbed out of the car and hobbled into the emergency room. "We've just been in an accident!" Luke called to the receptionist, as he guided me into a seat.

"I'm so sorry," he whispered, bloody arms wrapped tightly around me. "For everything. I love you."

I nodded and sobbed in his arms.

In moments, the door swung open. A whirlwhind of chaos. Nurses, doctors, shouting and running. A nurse guided me into a gurney—Luke, into a separate one. "I can walk," I protested, feebly. The woman in blue-green scrubs shook her head.

"Just in case."

She patted me on the shoulder and began pushing me down the hallway. The wheels rolled underneath me, smoothly clicking across the tile. The white lights flashed above me, blindingly bright.

Then I saw it.

A shadow. Just a flicker, in the corner of my eye, right behind the nurse. I tried to turn my head towards it.

A pulse of pain shot through my neck.

"Rest, dear," the nurse cooed, as she pushed me forward.

"Luke?" I whispered. He didn't hear me.

Click-click-click.

The gurney continued down the hallway. I turned towards the wall, watching the wallpaper. Blue and green triangles, overlapping and intersecting. Studying it helped my mind focus. Relax.

You're not in the car anymore. Whoever — whatever — that was is gone.

"Just rest," the nurse said softly, brushing against my shoulder. *Slap, slap, slap* — her footsteps beat in my ears. I felt the strength drain from my body. *In a few seconds, you'll be out of this hallway. In a room, with a doctor, a nurse. They'll fix you up, and...*

An acrid, rotten stench filled my nose.

My eyes flew open.

A silhouette. To the right of the gurney, matching our speed. I turned towards it—and it flit into my peripheral vision.

Into my blind spot.

I screamed. Over and over, I screamed. Patches of black shimmered in my vision, spreading until I could only see a pinprick of light from above.

Then everything went black.

**

I woke up in a hospital bed.

Beside me, a nurse took my blood pressure, humming softly to herself. The cuff inflated and began to pinch.

"Oh, you're up," she said. "Good."

"Where's Luke?" I whipped around the room, which was empty except for the two of us. "Is he—"

"He's in the next room," she said, ripping the cuff off. "And you both seem to be doing fine, now. Pressure's good, heart rate's good."

"What happened?"

"The strangest thing. You and your husband both suffered heart attacks—at the exact same time." She folded the cuff and replaced it in her cart. "If you hadn't been here, inside a hospital... I'm not sure you would've made it."

Images of the silhouette flashed through my mind, and I shuddered.

"I'm glad you're okay. The doctor will be in to see you, soon."

She bustled back into the hallway, leaving me alone.

We were discharged from the hospital later that day. Luke and I paid for a taxi back home, and spent hours just cuddling and enjoying each other's company. Suddenly, all the fighting, all the money troubles... they were insignificant.

We were alive.

And that's all that mattered.

"What should we do with the car?" I asked, pulling a hand through his hair.

"Junk it. Get one of those compactors to crush it up like a tin can."

I laughed. "Sounds good to me."

That's exactly what we did. That car is crushed up somewhere in a junkyard, now. Maybe whatever followed it was destroyed; or maybe it's trapped there. Either way—we're safe.

With what little money remained, we bought a decades-old used SUV. Luke didn't complain once about the dents, the smell, or the sputtering noise it made when it climbed steep hills.

Because we only had one requirement for our new car.

No blind spot detector.

HOW DO WE FALL ASLEEP?

We never remember the exact moment we fall asleep.

Sure, we remember the minutes *leading up to* that moment. Reciting our grocery list, listening to our spouse snore, replaying an embarrassing moment that happened ten years ago. But can you recall the exact moment you fell asleep last night?

Or how it happened?

I've always found this odd. We remember when we wake up, and sometimes, we even know the reason. A bad dream, a car honking outside.

But how do we *fall* asleep?

What happens in that magical moment, that pushes us into dreamland?

Nobody knows. It's a mystery. A little black hole in our memory.

That's why I decided to conduct a study.

My husband thought I was weird. "So you're setting an alarm on your phone, to go off every five minutes, as you fall asleep. Why?"

"Because it'll wake me up as I'm falling asleep."

"I don't get it."

"I want to know exactly when I fall asleep each night. And how."

"I still don't get it."

"I didn't expect you to."

Eric raised an eyebrow at me. "Is that supposed to be some sort of insult?"

"Maybe."

He laughed. "Okay. You do your thing. But can you do it in the guest room? I don't want to wake up every five minutes."

"Of course."

That night, at midnight, I lay on the twin bed in the guest room. My alarms were set. I was ready.

Brrring. The first alarm went off at 12:05. I was still pretty awake. The image that lingered in my mind was of our backyard—and what it would look like after the patio work was done.

I rolled over and closed my eyes.

Brrring. 12:10. Sleepier this time. Had I remembered to buy peas? I could... I could go to the store tomorrow, before my meeting...

Brrring. Barely awake. Peas and patio tiles melted into each other. I wondered, if I planted some peas in the morning, would they be ready by dinnertime?

Brrring.

Bingo.

Before I opened my eyes, I knew this was it. My thoughts were nonsense. Heavy fatigue immobilized my body. I was just barely asleep.

But something felt... *wrong*. It was more than just fatigue keeping my body still. I felt pressure on my chest, as if a dresser had been pulled on top of it. And my forehead stung, as if someone was pinching it.

My eyes flew open.

A black shadow sat on my chest. Green eyes smoldered in the darkness. Its mouth—if you could call it that—was long and tubular. It connected to my forehead, making a wet, sucking noise.

Get it off. Get it off!

I thrashed against the creature. The weight on my chest shifted. *Plop!* The mouth popped off my forehead.

At that same instant, the fog of sleep lifted. My thoughts were clear. My movements were nimble, quick.

And the creature was gone.

I ran down the hallway, my feet pounding against the carpet. "Eric!" I screamed, throwing his door open.

He slept peacefully. Completely unaware of the invisible creature that sat on his chest. Feeding on his energy. His thoughts.

I grabbed his shoulders and shook him awake. "Eric!" I screamed. "Wake up!"

His eyes slowly fluttered open.

"What's wrong?" he slurred, pulling himself up. I imagined the creature on top of him disengaging, causing him to wake up. Even though I couldn't see it—I knew it was there.

I knew.

"I saw it. The creature. It sits on our chest and sucks out our thoughts—our energy—like some sort of parasite—"

"What are you talking about?"

"It *causes* sleep! As soon as it stopped, I woke up. It *causes* sleep! It's black and shadowy and—"

"That sounds like sleep paralysis." He wrapped his arms around me and pulled me into a tight hug. "I'm so sorry. I know it can be terrifying. But it isn't real."

"It wasn't sleep paralysis, Eric! It's—"

"A nightmare, then. But don't worry. You're safe with me."

He pulled me tighter, rocking me gently as if I were a child. Tears streamed down my face, as the pieces fit together in my mind.

Sleep isn't some restorative function, encoded in our DNA. This creature—this *thing*—causes it. So it can feed on our thoughts, our energy. Like some sort of parasite.

A parasite that has existed since the beginning of time. Living with us, evolving with us, present in every country. Every home. Every bedroom.

We just never see it.

Because no one remembers how they fall asleep.

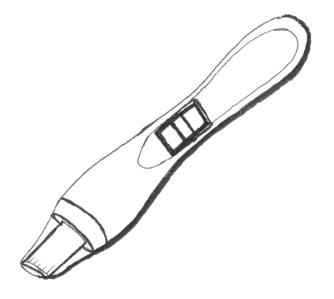

TWO PINK LINES

I am not pregnant.

I know I'm not. I just had my period a week ago. I have no morning sickness, no growing bump, nothing at all.

But my husband insists that I am.

Last night, we were sitting in the family room after dinner. I was sipping a glass of expensive red wine, when he suddenly turned to me and shouted: "What are you doing?"

"Drinking wine?"

"What? You're going to hurt the baby!"

Then he walked over—and snatched the glass out of my hands.

"Hey!"

"You know you shouldn't be drinking while pregnant."

"What?! I'm not pregnant." I reached for the glass; he yanked it out of my reach.

"Elisabeth. Please. You're going to hurt the baby."
He ran over to the sink, dumped out the wine, and set
the empty glass on the counter with an *angry clink.* Then
he ran over and pressed a hand to my forehead. "You
feel hot. I should call the doctor."

"Michael—"

He ran out of the room.

This must be some crazy prank, I thought. *Well,
whatever it is—it's not very funny.* Within a few minutes,
Michael came back, and pressed the phone to my ear.

"Elisabeth?"

Dr. Jones's voice came over the line. My primary
care physician.

I stared up at Michael. *Seriously?* I mouthed at him. I
was sure Dr. Jones doesn't appreciate late-night calls
about... whatever this nonsense was.

"Uh, yes, it's me," I said, uneasily.

"Michael tells me you drank wine tonight. You *know*
that can cause fetal alcohol syndrome."

"Dr. Jones, I'm not pregnant."

"Right. And I'm not a doctor!" he replied,
sarcastically. "Now, a fever isn't good, either. If your
temperature goes above 99.5F, give me a call, okay?"

I glanced at Michael. He was staring down at me,
with an expression on his face that was a mixture of
concern and judgement. "Uh, okay, Dr. Jones."

"Thank you, Elisabeth."

The call ended.

"So you heard it from the doctor himself," Michael said, taking his phone back from me. "No wine. If the fever gets worse, we call him. Okay?"

"Michael... I'm *not* pregnant." I stood up. "I don't know why you, and Dr. Jones, think I am. I'm not. I just had my period a week ago—"

"You had bleeding? That could be very, very dangerous for the baby! Why didn't you tell me?!"

I stood up and got in his face. "What is *wrong* with you? I. Am. Not. Pregnant!"

"Elisabeth—" he walked towards me, and gently pressed his hands on my belly— "the stress isn't good for her."

"*Her?!*"

"The baby."

"There. Is. No. Baby!"

"Okay. Elisabeth. Look. You're clearly having some sort of..." I knew the words 'mental breakdown' were probably on his tongue, but instead, he said "problem. But here, I'll show you."

He disappeared upstairs for a few minutes. When he came back, he was holding a pregnancy test. He pushed it into my hands.

"Go ahead and see for yourself."

"Fine."

I closed the door, locked it, and strode over to the toilet. I ripped open the foil packaging, pulled the cap off, and held it under the stream of urine.

1... 2... 3...

I set my phone timer to count the minutes until the results were ready. Then I closed my eyes. *This is so stupid. I'm not pregnant.* I couldn't even remember the last time Michael and I had unprotected sex.

I frowned. *Why would we even be using protection if I'm pregnant?* Another thing that made no sense. *This is all some weird joke. It has to be...*

Beep. Beep. Beep. The timer was done.

I opened my eyes. With trembling hands, I brought the test up to my face.

Two pink lines.

Positive.

The strength drained from my legs. My heart pounded in my chest, and the room began to spin. *Pregnant.*

"Michael," I stuttered, handing him the test. My hands subconsciously drifted to my belly. I held them there firmly. *Is there really a baby in there?* "You're right. I'm pregnant. But I... I was bleeding. Just a few days ago."

"We need to call Dr. Jones. Right now. The baby could be..." He didn't finish the sentence, grabbing his phone from the nightstand.

"But if I tested positive, don't we know that the baby—"

"No. HCG levels can stay elevated even after... the miscarriage." He pressed the phone to his ear.

I crumpled on the bed and began to cry.

What the hell is going on?!

Michael and I had been married for three years—and before this moment, every day of it had been bliss. He was always kind, thoughtful. He bought us a beautiful, 5000-square-foot mansion here in the countryside. He even cooked me dinner some nights after work—pastas, pies, pastries. Then he'd tuck me in and let me fall asleep while he did the dishes.

Now, it felt like all of that was crumbling down.

***

"See that? That's the baby."

Dr. Jones pointed to the screen, as he pressed the probe to my belly. "You didn't miscarry. She—or he—is okay."

I stared at the screen in disbelief.

"How... how far along am I?"

"About six weeks."

"*Six weeks?!*" I sat up on the table. Glanced from Michael to Dr. Jones. "I don't... even remember finding out that I was pregnant. Or telling you. Or Michael."

He ignored my comment. "Bleeding can be a bad sign. I'm going to prescribe one month of bedrest to reduce the chances of miscarriage."

"Bedrest?!"

Before Dr. Jones could reply, Michael wrapped an arm around my shoulders. "Let's go home. We'll get you a nice snack and some good TV, okay?"

I nodded.

But my entire body felt numb.

Michael took me back home. He set me up in one of our many guest bedrooms with snacks, water, and even one of our flat-screen TVs. After he connected it, he fiddled with something on top of the nightstand.

"What's that?" I asked. His body blocked my view.

"Just organizing all your things," he said. When he pulled away, my chapstick, sparkling water, and phone were lined up perfectly. "Now, would you like me to get you some chocolate, or—"

"I think I'll just go to bed. It's been a long day."

"Okay, Elisabeth." He walked towards the door and flicked out the light. "I love you."

"I love you, too."

When he left, I grabbed the bottle of sparkling water—a terrible consolation prize compared to the wine—and watched the old movie playing on TV. Some black-and-white film with Ingrid Bergman.

Soon I was asleep.

***

The next morning—Saturday—I woke up early. With Michael still asleep, I snuck out of the room and into the bathroom. As I peeled off my clothes and started the shower water, I caught my reflection in the mirror.

I am not pregnant.

Am I?

The water was hot on my skin. I scrubbed furiously, as if trying to scrub the memories of last night away. *Just some joke,* I told myself, again. *It's just some stupid joke.* I towel-dried my hair, walked across the marble floor, and opened the bathroom door.

Michael stood right in the doorway. Inches from the door. Every muscle in his face was taut.

"What were you doing?" he asked.

"Showering," I replied, uneasily.

His face relaxed. "That's great," he said, leaving me and walking over to our immense closet. "I found a great outfit for you to wear today." He stepped out carrying an unfamiliar mint-green top, cinched underneath the bust.

He gave it to me, and I saw the tag: *Pea in the Pod.*

Maternity clothes.

"I... I think I'd be more comfortable in a T-shirt," I said.

"Sure." He went back into the closet and retrieved my oversized Kirby T-shirt. "Now, will you be okay here by yourself, for the next few hours?"

"You're going somewhere?"

"We were supposed to meet Caylinn and Thomas for brunch. Remember? I've already told them you aren't feeling well, but that I'd be there."

"Oh."

Secretly, I was thrilled. I hated Caylinn and her stupid fake teeth and five-carat engagement ring. And the way she laughed so daintily, with her hand over her mouth and her eyes all sparkly.

And, more importantly... I still felt like none of this was adding up. I wanted time, *alone,* to process things for myself.

He helped me into the guest room and turned on the TV for me. "I love you," he said, kissing me on the forehead.

I waited until I heard the rumble of the engine and the tires roll against the wet road. Then I grabbed my phone off the nightstand—and dialed my mom.

I tell my mom everything, in real time. She'd be able to give an exact timeline of when everything happened. The pregnancy. Everything else.

Brzt. Brzt. Brzt.

A busy signal erupted in my ears.

My heart began to pound. I pulled my phone from my ear and dialed my sister. A few of my friends. Even my estranged dad.

Every single number led to a busy signal.

Hands shaking, I dialed Michael's number. It rang twice—then went to voicemail.

This isn't right.

I replaced my phone on the nightstand.

That's when I saw it.

A tiny, blinking red light. Just an inch or so underneath the edge of the lampshade. I leaned over and looked up.

A black lens blinked back at me.

What the hell?

A camera?

I grabbed my bottle of sparkling water and carefully placed it in front of the lens. When I was sure it was blocked, I slowly pulled myself out of bed. I gently walked across the hall. Then down the stairs.

I grabbed my keys off the rack, got in the car, and drove right to CVS.

I'm going to get to the bottom of this.

I ran inside and grabbed a pregnancy test off the shelf. Then I was running to the store bathroom. Ripping through the foil. The floor was sticky, and the place stunk of urine, but I hardly noticed.

I used the test, re-capped it, and waited.

3 minutes. 3 agonizing minutes.

Then I opened my eyes.

One line.

Not pregnant.

Relief flooded through me. I pulled up my pants, threw the test in the trash, and headed out into the store. The aisles blurred through my tears, the ground felt wobbly under my feet; but I somehow made it into the car.

Then I bawled my eyes out.

What the hell is going on?

He must have messed with the first pregnancy test.

He knew I wouldn't believe him. That a positive test was the only thing that would convince me. *But... why?*

Why lie to me? Deceive me?

My phone buzzed in my pocket. I jumped, then pulled it out. *Michael.* My heart dropped. I set it on the passenger seat, unwilling to answer.

But then he called again.

And again.

And again. The fifth time, I picked up, my hands shaking.

"Elisabeth? Where are you?"

He sounded angry. Sure, his voice was restrained, but I could feel the undercurrent of rage ready to break free at any moment.

I steadied my voice. "I just... went to Trader Joe's. For some chocolate." It didn't sound very convincing.

"You're on bedrest, Elisabeth," he said, his voice slightly calmer. "You're not supposed to be out and about. You could miscarry our baby."

I fought back the sobs.

"Come home. Right now."

"Okay," I lied. "I'm on my way back."

I pulled out of the parking lot. But instead of turning left, towards home—I turned right. I didn't know where I was going. But any place was better than "home."

Brzt.

My phone buzzed in my pocket. *Michael.* I picked it up.

"You lied," he growled.

"Michael—what?"

"You lied. You're not going home."

The words sent a shiver down my spine. I glanced around the car—was it a webcam? A GPS tracker?

"I am. The street's too busy to make a left. I made a right and I'm going to turn around."

Better to play it safe. Pretend I didn't know what he was up to. I pulled into a parking lot to "turn around," then picked the phone back up and dialed 911.

All I got was a busy signal.

"Dammit," I grumbled, throwing the phone on the seat. I'd have to do this the old-fashioned way—drive right over to the police station. I started the car and began to pull out.

No.

A familiar, silver SUV was pulling into the parking lot.

Michael's car.

I pressed on the gas. The car lurched forward, and I swung towards him. With a screech of tires, he pulled forward.

Blocking the only exit to the parking lot.

Then the door swung open as he got out of the car. He charged towards me, eyes flashing in anger.

I pulled forward—and shot over the grass.

The car jostled wildly. Horns honked as I pulled onto the street. "Elisabeth!" I heard him shout behind me.

But he was too late.

***

It's been a year, and I still don't know why Michael did it.

I don't know why the man I married three years ago—the man I fell madly in love with at only twenty-two—suddenly wanted to control every aspect of my life. To deceive me into thinking I was pregnant.

The police arrested Dr. Jones. He was never really a doctor—just a friend of Michael's. He'd been my "primary care physician" since we got married and moved out here a few years ago. Now that I thought about it, it made sense—while he had equipment and an office space, he never prescribed me any medicine or ordered any bloodwork.

And the "ultrasound" he showed me? Just a video clip he got from YouTube.

So Dr. Jones is locked up and facing time for everything he did. Michael, however... is still out there. By the time the police arrived at our home, most of the evidence was gone. The fake pregnancy test, the webcam—all gone. The only thing I had to show for it was the GPS tracker they eventually found in my car. And I can't prove *he's* the one who put it here.

Without evidence, they were forced to let him go.

I live across the country, now, several hundred miles away from where we built our life. I changed my name. I live in a small house, and make my living working at the local library. It's a modest life—a far cry from what we had.

But I am free of him.

And that's what matters the most.

SUPERSTITIOUS

My grandmother is superstitious.

It was only when lived with her for the summer that I realized how bad it had gotten. She had this huge freakin' list taped to the fridge, with ten different "rules" she has to abide by.

And she was making me follow them, too.

When I opened my umbrella inside, she grabbed my arm and yanked me back. "Don't open the umbrella inside! Didn't you see the rules?"

"Oh, sorry. I thought those rules were, uh, just for you."

"No. *Everyone* who lives here must obey the rules," she said, in raspy whisper.

It made me really sad. Once Grandma Jan was sharp as a needle—a grounded, logical person who *occasionally* bought into superstitions and the paranormal. A rabbit's foot here, a penny there. Now it seemed, in her late 80s, that part of her had grown and grown until it subsumed everything else.

With a heavy heart, I walked over to the fridge and read the rules.

1. Do not spill salt.
2. Do not open umbrellas inside.
3. Do not put on clothes inside-out.
4. Do not clip fingernails after dark.
5. Do not break any mirrors.

Mostly common superstitions, though the fingernail one was weird. I continued reading, with difficulty—her handwriting grew messier, more frenzied.

6. Do not look in the mirror while wearing black.
7. Do not whistle inside the house.
8. If you wake up to see your bedroom door open, do not close it. Likewise, if you see the attic stairs pulled down, do not push them back up.
9. Never let the refrigerator go empty. Always have enough to make an offering.
10. Keep the curtains closed after 10 PM. Do not open them again until 6 AM.

I wanted to tell her it was a whole lot of hogwash. But then I realized it was probably a bad idea to upset her at such an old age.

"No problem, Grandma. I'll follow the rules."

Yeah, right.

She put me in the spare bedroom, down the hall from her. It was a small thing, furnished with only a twin bed and a tiny desk. But I couldn't complain—it was either this, for free, or an apartment, for $1000+ a month.

But of course, the money wasn't the main reason I was here. My grandma probably wouldn't be around much longer. According to my mom, she kept getting these random bruises, and doctors were worried she had a blood disorder. And some other stuff I couldn't pronounce. I wanted to spend all the time I could with her—she was still my grandma. Still the one that comforted me when my first cat died, still the one who taught me how to bake the most amazing snickerdoodles.

I loved her even if I had to put up with some weird-ass rules.

"I'm going to bed," she said, as she passed by my room that night. "Sleep well, Chrissy. I love you."

"Goodnight, Grandma. I love you too."

I spent an hour on the internet, then put away my computer and fell asleep.

***

I woke up a few hours later. Groaning in the darkness, I rolled over—to see my bedroom door open.

I didn't leave that open. I stared at it, half-asleep, too tired to get up and close it. *Ah, well. According to the RULES, I can't close it anyway.*

I snuggled up to my pillow and closed my eyes.

That's when I heard the whistling.

A soft, melancholy tune. Coming from downstairs.

Every muscle in my body froze. *That was one of the rules. Wasn't it? No whistling inside? …So why would Grandma be whistling downstairs? At—*I glanced at the clock—*freakin' 2 AM?*

I pulled myself out of bed and walked into the hallway. The attic stairs had been pulled down. The darkness from the attic bled down into the hallway, along with the faint smell of rust and rotten food. Behind it, Grandma's door hung open.

I slowly descended the stairs. "Grandma?"

The whistling stopped.

When I entered the kitchen, it was empty. "Grandma? Where are you?"

"Over here."

I looked up to see Grandma appear from the dark family room, wearing her floral nightdress. "Did I wake you, honey? I'm so sorry. I wanted to get some milk for my heartburn."

"No, no, it's fine. I just thought you weren't supposed to whistle," I said, with a chuckle. "According to the rules..."

"You heard the whistling?" she asked, her eyes wide.

I nodded.

She grabbed my arm in a vice grip and led me back up the stairs. "Go back to sleep," she commanded. Before I could reply, she disappeared back down the hallway—leaving my door open.

***

"I think Grandma's going crazy."

"Oh, are you talking about her rules?" Mom said on the other end. "I know they're eccentric, but she gets really upset if you break them. And the doctor... he doesn't want us to upset her, you know?"

I sighed. "Isn't it bad for her mental health?"

"We all go a little crazy near the end. Uncle Finley though the government was tapping all his phones in his 90s. Great-Grandma Beasley always talked about some bat following her around. Just best to let sleeping dogs lie, at this point."

"But the rules are *so* weird, Mom. Like *really* freakin' weird. And I woke up last night at 2 AM to find the attic stairs pulled down! I mean, what was she doing?"

"You know what?" Mom said, a bit of anger tinging her voice. "She lives by herself in that secluded little house, 365 days a year. The only socialization she gets is her weekly trip to the grocery store, and monthly visits from your dad and me. Anyone would go a little nuts under those circumstances—even you. Lay off her, okay?"

"Fine."

So I followed the rules. I was a good girl and didn't open any umbrellas indoors, do any whistling, or break any mirrors. Sometimes I'd wake up to see my door open in the middle of the night, but I just ignored it and left it open. A few times, when I made my way to the bathroom, I whacked my head on the attic stairs that were pulled down. Once or twice I heard the whistling again, but I ignored that, too.

Mom was right. So Grandma was a little crazy. We're all a little crazy, aren't we? Maybe time just scratches away all the normalcy we hide under, and we're all batshit insane at the end.

Things were good as I accepted that reality.

Then Sunday happened.

I was watching Netflix when I heard a clink—then a shout. I threw my laptop on the bed and ran down the stairs. "Grandma!" I yelled, fearing the worst. "Grandma, are you okay?"

I found her standing over the kitchen table. Sobbing her eyes out. On the table was a salt-shaker, tipped over—next to a pile of spilled salt.

"I didn't mean—I just was cleaning up the plates and I—I—" She could barely make cohesive sentences through the sobs.

"Sssh, Grandma, it's okay! I'm going to clean it up, now."

I felt awful seeing Grandma like that. She was outright sobbing, her entire body shaking, as if she feared for her life. Over spilled salt.

I brought my palm up to the table's edge and brushed the salt into it with my other hand. I was so sad for Grandma, but I was also incredibly unnerved. Seeing someone you love, get so upset about something so trivial… it was disturbing.

"It's all clean. See?" I said, brushing off my hands. The salt rained down into the trash. "Nothing to worry about, Grandma."

Her sobs quieted, and she looked at me with red eyes. "But… he'll *know*," she said.

"What?"

"Even though you cleaned it up… he'll still know."

"Who?"

She looked at me. "The spirit of the house."

"The *spirit* of the house?" Despite how skeptical I was of ghosts, spirits, and everything paranormal, I felt a shiver go down my spine. Wasn't it legend that ghosts and spirits didn't like salt? That if you surrounded yourself with salt, you'd be protected from them? Propagating a superstition about spilling salt could be a ghost's defense mechanism.

If ghosts existed. Which they absolutely, positively did *not*.

That night I barely slept a wink. I stared at my ceiling as the minutes ticked by. 2 AM, 3 AM, 4 AM.

It was around 4:15 that I heard something stir.

Thump, thump, thump.

Soft footsteps from overhead. From the attic. Every muscle in my body froze as I listened to the steps migrate towards Grandma's end of the house.

Then—*creeeeaaaak*—the metallic whine of the attic stairs being pulled down.

Followed by footsteps.

I forced myself out of bed. It took a huge, heaping serving of courage to do so, but I did. When I finally got to the door and pulled it open, the hallway was empty.

Maybe the ghost is here, right now, staring at me. And I just don't know it.

No, no, shut up! Ghosts don't exist, you idiot!

The back of my neck prickled with the distinct, awful feeling of being watched. But rather than run back into my own room—believe me, I really wanted to—I ran over to check on Grandma. Her door hung open, as usual. "Grandma, are you okay?"

Her bed was empty.

"Grandma? Where are you?"

That's when I heard the soft sounds of sobbing below. I ran down the stairs, nearly slipping, and burst into the kitchen.

Grandma stood in the kitchen.

In front of her stood "the spirit of the house."

Not some dark, ethereal specter. Not some white, translucent ghost. A man, of flesh and blood. His brown beard was unkempt and messy, his blue eyes wild. He wore tattered clothes, black boots, and a yellow-toothed grin.

"You've broken the rules of the house," he whispered, stepping towards her. She flinched and took a step back.

"Please don't hurt me," she sobbed.

"I'm the man of the house. *I* make the rules." Grin growing wider, he raised his hand to smack her across the shoulder.

"No!" I shouted. I charged at him. We collided and fell to the ground. Terror—and relief—washed over my grandma's face.

"Call the police!" I shouted. "Now!"

He tried to wriggle underneath me. I grabbed the nearest thing—a chair, from the kitchen table—and smacked him as hard as I could in the head.

***

The man was a drifter by the name of Harold McCann.

According to the police, he'd snuck into my poor grandma's house over a year ago. They found his living space in the attic, complete with a makeshift bed over the rafters, books, and dishes that held my grandma's leftover food. The "offerings."

He'd slowly taken advantage of Grandma, persuading her over months to follow his "rules." He told her he was an angry spirit of the house, and in her sensitive, mentally fragile state, she believed him. He made her swear to tell nobody of his existence. And whenever she broke the rules, he hit her.

Hence the bruises.

My poor, poor grandma.

For the time being, she's moved in with me. We have a tiny little apartment near my college, and I've been helping her recover. She's doing well. She freaked out a little when I dropped a cosmetic mirror the other day, but overall, she's getting much better.

She even whistles inside the apartment, now—and it's the sweetest sound I've ever heard.

OUT FOR DELIVERY

It all started with a *ding*.

I checked my phone to see the notification: *Your package is arriving today.*

I stared at it, confused. I hadn't ordered anything off Amazon recently. In fact, I thought I'd uninstalled the app from my phone, in an attempt to save myself from 1 AM impulse buys of weird kitchen gadgets I didn't need.

"Hey Ben," I said, "did you buy something off Amazon?"

"Yeah. Socks, a colander, and a... what was it... oh! Those little rings that hold up shower curtains, with the metal beads on them—"

"No, that was last week. I'm talking about today. There's a package arriving."

He furrowed his eyebrows. "Oh. No, I didn't order anything since then. Did you?"

"No. That's why I'm asking you."

He frowned. "Maybe Alexa ordered something by mistake."

"Does that happen?"

"Yeah. A lot of people complain about it online."

Of course. Another way for Amazon to reel in money — by making 'mistake' orders. *Whoops, you just spent $102.71 on a new stainless steel frying pan!* With a huff, I pulled out my computer.

I went to Amazon. Clicked *Orders*. There it was — an item, ordered a few days ago.

But tshe product image was replaced with the standard gray text: *no image available*. The price box read "$0.00". The title of the product read: *[Unknown]*. Underneath, in green, bold letters, it read:

Arriving today by 8pm.

"Hey, Ben? Look at this."

His eyes glanced over the computer screen. "Oooh, that's so weird. Probably just a glitch." He looked at me, and I must've looked pretty upset, because he added: "I wouldn't worry about it, Ellie."

I waited for the doorbell to ring. Every time I heard the slightest thump or scuffling sound outside, I jumped and peered out the window to see if the package had arrived. But the afternoon passed without event. As the time approached 8 PM—and the package still hadn't arrived—I felt both disappointment and relief.

I'd been excited to see what the mystery package was. But also a bit freaked out over what appeared to be some sort of phantom Amazon order.

But I guess it *was* a glitch. There never was any package that would be delivered. It was just an error in the system.

Then, at 7:46 PM, my phone dinged.

Your package has arrived!

I jumped off the couch and ran to the door, as fast as my feet would take me. "You okay?" Ben called, holding a cold slice of pizza.

"The package is here!"

"Oooh!" he said, through a mouthful of congealed cheese. "I thought it was just a digital glitch. But if they actually sent us a package we didn't pay for—awesome! Free stuff!"

"It's not awesome. It's *weird.*"

He followed me to the door, practically dancing. My hand fell on the knob, shaking. *I shouldn't be nervous*, I scolded myself. *Mail mix-ups happen all the time. Ben's right—this is good. It's free stuff. Free stuff is always good.*

I yanked the door open.

There it was. A brown box, about a foot on a side, sealed shut with blue tape. I bent over and picked it up. It was much heavier than I expected.

"Here. I'll take it," Ben said. We brought it to the kitchen, set it down on the island. He grabbed a butter knife. "Ready?" he asked.

"I guess."

He plunged it through the tape. Pulled open the flaps.

"What the hell?!" he said, backing away from it.

It was empty.

I was staring at ordinary cardboard. Slightly frayed and bent in places, held together with that blue tape. I circled around the island, staring inside, as if something might suddenly materialize out of thin air. "But it was so heavy," I finally said. "How could it be empty?"

"I thought it was going to be something really good. Like a boom box," Ben replied, sadly.

"A boom box? What is this, the '90s?"

He laughed. "Hey. I would've been happy."

He disappeared back into the living room. I grabbed the box and lifted it. It was light, now. Normal. As my heart slowed, I folded the box up and tossed it in the recycle bin.

All that fuss over an empty box.

***

I woke up cold.

I squinted at the clock. 3:34 AM. The window was wide open, curtains billowing in the breeze. "Dammit," I said, rushing up to close it.

That's when I noticed the bed was empty.

"Ben?" I whispered. I glanced at the bathroom; the light was off. The bedroom door hung wide open, though—and a dim, golden light shone across the stairs.

He was downstairs.

I walked out into the hallway. It was even colder out here. I whipped around, and noticed *every* bedroom door was open. And inside each, every window was open.

What kind of fuckery is Ben up to?

"Ben!" I shouted.

No reply.

I sighed and started down the stairs. As I descended, I started to hear it: *Schrp. Schrp. Schrp.* A repeated, metallic noise that throbbed in my ears like a heartbeat. "Dammit, Ben!" I called loudly. "What the hell are you —"

I froze.

Ben was standing at the kitchen island. Hunched over something. He didn't look up at me; his arm just moved back and forth, almost mechanically.

He was sharpening knives.

Every single knife we owned was divided into two piles on either side of him. *Schrip, schrip* — he pulled that knife out of the sharpener and placed it in the right pile with a metallic *clang*. Then he picked up the next one, a 12-inch long chef's knife, and began sharpening that.

And then he stopped.

I ducked behind the wall. Holding a hand over my mouth.

"Ellie?" he called from the kitchen.

My lungs felt like they would burst.

"I have something to show you," he said. His voice was flat – almost monotone. His bare feet slapped against the tile, slowly, heavily, as he walked towards me.

I took in a slow, shuddering breath. Extended my foot out in front of me, silently.

"Ellie?"

I ran.

I took off, down the hall. My feet slipped against the linoleum but I forced myself forward, lungs burning. "Ellie!" he screamed.

His voice was no longer light and kind.

It was angry.

I grabbed the keys off the hook. Then I opened the garage and ran out into the driveway. His hulking form was silhouetted in the doorway. The knife gripped tightly in his hand.

I dove into the car. Locked the doors, started it up. The headlights washed over him, and his eyes glinted eerily in the light.

For a moment he was still.

Then he ran towards the car. As fast as he possibly could. Knife raised in his hand. Mouth open in an animalistic howl.

I peeled out of the driveway.

My mind raced. Ben had never been violent – never. *Maybe it wasn't what it looked like. Somehow, he was innocent, and I let my fears get the worst of me.* I knew it was impossible. That there was no other explanation.

I just didn't want to accept it.

It wasn't until I pulled into the police station that I remembered the empty package. So heavy when we lifted it from the doorstep. So light, after Ben opened it.

Maybe the box wasn't empty at all.

Maybe there was something inside. Something we couldn't see.

And we just let it free.

FEED

I've been a detective for 18 years.

The death of Natalia Johns was the most disturbing case I'd ever seen. More disturbing than the hit-and-run last year that I'd lost weeks of sleep over, *and* the man that had been living in an old woman's attic for a year.

"Natalia Johns, 20 years old," Barry said, sitting down with a groan. His potbelly brushed against my desk, knocking one of my pens on the floor. "For now, it's labeled a suicide—but I'll be damned if that's the truth."

"...Okay," I said, hesitantly. "What was the cause of death?"

"Dehydration."

"And that was *suicide*?"

"Well, what else would we call it? She was found alone, in her apartment, sitting on her bed." He lowered his voice to a whisper. "But get this. The coroner's report says her eyes were all dried up. As if she hadn't blinked. For *hours*."

Despite the warm room, I felt a chill go down my spine.

"No one can willfully resist blinking for *hours,* Joe. It's not a suicide. Absolutely not."

"So you think someone broke in, somehow, and killed her."

"Not exactly. No signs of forced entry, and her door was locked from the inside." He grabbed a chocolate from my candy bowl and greedily unwrapped it. "Ah, damn, I love these things."

I stared at him from across the desk. *How can he eat when we're talking about... this?*

"There was other weird stuff, too," he said, through a mouth full of chocolate. "Based on the report, it looks like she didn't leave her bed in the 24 hours leading up to her death. The muscles in her thumb were kind of wrecked. If you ask me—and I know you're not asking, but *if* you were—I'd say it was some weird-ass torture."

"By who? An ex-boyfriend?"

"Yeah. I think some ex-boyfriend still had a key her apartment. He broke in one night, tortured her, tied her up, let her die of dehydration."

"But the body wasn't tied up."

"No."

"Was there any sign of sexual assault?"

"No."

"How about fingerprints? Or—"

"Okay, I get it!" he said, standing up. "My theory's crappy. But you know what's an even crappier theory?

Suicide." He got up and shuffled over to the door. "Take a look at the file. Tell me what *you* think."

The door shut.

I opened the manila folder. A young woman's face stared back up at me. Auburn hair, dark eyes, a thin face that tapered into a pointed chin.

My heart sank as I looked at her. *How her parents must feel.* My daughter was 16. I couldn't fathom how horrible it must be to lose a child.

I set her photo aside and continued through the report. It was as Barry described it: a strange, disturbing case that definitely didn't sound like a suicide.

That night, I picked at my dinner. My wife looked across the table at me, frowning. "Is everything okay, Joe?"

"Just work," I replied, not wanting to discuss the details in front of Maddie or Josh.

"Maddie got an A- on her history test today."

"That's great!" I said, with as much enthusiasm as I could muster.

"Thanks, Mom," Maddie sighed. "Now I feel like even more of a nerd."

As soon as dinner was over, I went into my study, grabbed my laptop, and continued what I'd started at the office—a full-out search on Natalia Johns. After several minutes of scrolling through random athletic articles (she played soccer in college, apparently), I found her social media accounts.

They were scrubbed clean.

Weird. I didn't see that in the report. I clicked over to an internet archiver—the type that saves previous versions of websites—and pasted in her Instagram URL.

Natalia Johns. 16,503 posts. 1,067 followers. 972 following.

Wow. That's a LOT of posts.

Maybe that was normal, though. Even Maddie spent a few hours a day on social media. Her posts were constantly in my Facebook newsfeed. At least three a day.

Still. Three a day would come out to fifteen *years* of posts... and Instagram's only been around for nine. At least, assuming I did the math right on my phone's calculator.

I scrolled down.

My heart stopped.

They were selfies. Dozens of them. Natalia staring blankly at the camera, her face pale. Deep bags under her eyes. Sunlight streaming over her face from the nearby window, shining through her tangled hair. The photos were nearly identical—only the slight tilt of her head, or a hair out of place, differentiated them.

I clicked on the first one.

The description was just a long list of hashtags. #selfie, #nofilter, #nomakeup... you know, the usual hashtags young women use on their photos. The post had no comments, but over six thousand likes. Strange for someone with only a thousand followers.

I glanced down. It was posted October 18th.

The day she died.

I scrolled through the rest of the posts—all dated the day she died. After about a hundred or so, the photos darkened as the sun set.

After scrolling through *hundreds,* I finally came upon a post dated October 17th. Then I scrolled back up, counted the rows and columns of photos, and did some quick multiplication.

There were over a thousand photos posted on the day she died.

How the hell did she make a thousand posts in ONE day? That'd come out to a little less than one a minute, according to the calculator.

Maybe she automatically scheduled the posts. But why? Why would she post nearly a thousand selfies of herself? And why would she stay up all night, snapping one every minute?

But if she didn't schedule them...

Some of the case details would make perfect sense. She wouldn't have time to eat, sleep, or drink, if she were glued to her phone making all these posts.

"Aren't you going to say goodnight to Josh and Maddie?"

I looked up to see Shannon standing in the doorway, arms crossed. "Sure," I said, setting the laptop aside. I walked into the hallway and poked my head into Josh's room.

"Goodnight."

He barely looked up from his tablet. "Goodnight, Dad," he muttered.

"Goodnight, Maddie. Congrats on your test."

She didn't even look up from her phone. "Goodnight, Dad."

I walked back to the bedroom and grabbed my laptop. Somehow, the Instagram page had closed out, and it was back on my personal Facebook tab. I scrolled through my newsfeed for a minute, but it was all garbage. A photo of my brother catching a fish. Someone asking for handyman recommendations. A photo of Maddie in her pirate costume.

I closed the laptop and set it on the nightstand. After an hour of tossing and turning, I finally fell asleep.

***

"There's something wrong with her social media."

Barry frowned across from me. "Oh, yeah. Her accounts were wiped, right? Sorry. I forgot about that part."

"It's worse than that. I found her posts and... it's not good." I pulled out my laptop and turned it towards him.

Barry furled his eyebrows. "Why did she upload so many copies of the same photo?"

"It's not the same photo. Each one is a new, individual selfie. And she posted *all* of these—" I scrolled down— "the day she died. "

"This is insane," he said, clicking through the posts. "Okay. New theory. Her ex-boyfriend comes in with the spare key. Forces her, at gunpoint, to take selfies and upload them."

"There's no gun in the photo."

"It could be out of frame."

I sighed, and turned the laptop back to me. "I don't know, Barry. What would the motive be? To make someone take a thousand selfies?"

"Torture."

I raised my eyebrows. "Selfie torture? Okay. Sure. That sounds *so* plausible."

"You have a better explanation?"

"Not yet."

We gave all of the information to our tech team. They dove in, looking into her social media accounts and examining her phone. By the end of the day, the only suspicious thing they found was a post from one of Natalia's friends.

It was a strange series of symbols and dashes that ran for about five lines. It was posted by Natalia's friend from high school, Melissa, a few days before she died. Natalia had liked it—so she'd definitely seen it in her newsfeed.

They hadn't figured out exactly what it meant, yet, but they had their suspicions. "It could be an encoded message," the tech woman said. "Or a trigger of some kind. We'll be working on it."

The post—just like Natalia's selfies—had a disproportionate number of likes.

Barry and I both thought, at this point, someone else was involved. Maybe an ex-boyfriend, maybe someone else. Maybe the person wasn't even physically there, but messaging her online. Her phone was being analyzed by the experts. All we could do was wait for answers.

When I got home, the dinner table was already set— but only Josh and Shannon were seated. "Where's Maddie?" I asked, hanging up my coat.

"She's in her room, I think," Shannon said, rolling her eyes. "Won't come down. I figured you'd have better luck."

Oh, great. I get to be the bad guy. I trudged up the stairs and knocked on her door. "Maddie! Dinner time!"

No reply.

"Hey Maddie, come on! We're all waiting for you!"

Silence.

Okay. I don't like to barge in like this, but she's not cooperating. "I'm coming in!" I said. After a few seconds of silence ticked by, I opened the door.

Maddie sat in her chair. Facing away from me.

"Maddie?"

I stepped up to her, and then I realized: she was staring at her phone, laying in her lap.

"Maddie. Hey. It's dinner time." I crouched next to her. She didn't even glance in my direction. She just stared at her phone.

Not even blinking.

Then she raised it and turned the camera on herself. *Snap.*

"Maddie?"

She ignored me, fingers racing against the screen.

I began to panic. Heart pounding, I reached over and grabbed the phone out of her hands. "Maddie! Look at me!"

For a second, she did.

Then she leapt at me, a wild look in her eyes. Clawing for the phone. "Maddie! Stop!" I stretched my arm up, keeping the phone out of her reach. Her fingers raked against my arm, nails digging into me.

And then she shrieked.

It was like no noise I'd ever heard her make before. An animalistic howl, like she'd lost every bit of judgment, of intelligent thought, of humanity. Just a cry of pure anguish with no rhyme or reason to it.

With all my might, I threw the phone on the floor.

Then—before she could get it—I brought my foot down on it. Hard.

CRACK.

The screen snapped under my feet.

Maddie froze.

Her blank stare turned into a look of terror and confusion. Her lip began to tremble. "Dad... I'm so sorry... I don't..." She trailed off, and began to cry.

"What happened?" I asked, fearing I already knew the answer.

"I don't know. I... I just kept taking photos. And posting them. Over and over. I kept thinking, I want people to see me, I want them to see this photo. But then, when you took the phone away, I... don't know."

"It's okay." I wrapped her in a hug. "It's all okay, now, Maddie."

But inside, I was terrified. *Is that what Natalia experienced?*

Would Maddie be dead in a few days, if she were living alone?

"Do you remember what you were doing before that happened?" I asked, softly. "Before you started taking the photos?"

"I... I was scrolling through Facebook. Looking at some dumb Halloween photos, something you posted, and—"

"Something *I* posted?"

"Yeah. You posted this weird thing with symbols and stuff."

I let go. Raced over to my laptop, pulled up Facebook. Sure enough—there was status update "I" had posted yesterday. That I had no memory of posting. Strange symbols, ellipses, dashes.

Identical to the post Natalia's friend had made.

I glanced down, and my heart plummeted.

The post already had 157 likes.

***

It's been a week. Maddie is fine, now, and I've been checking in with every person who saw my post. Thankfully, most of them don't live alone. Their spouses have strict instructions to watch for symptoms, and destroy phones if necessary.

But more cases like Natalia's have popped up all over the country. People dying of dehydration, alone, leaving nothing but a trail of social media posts behind. For some, it's selfies; for others, it's sharing memes, writing every passing thought in a status update, or posting endless "throwback" photos. The trigger of symbols continues to circulate around, spreading from friend to friend like some sort of digital virus.

Our police force hasn't determined much, yet. But they have determined one thing.

All the posts the "infected" create are transmitted to a server in an undisclosed location, before the accounts self-destruct and erase everything. Someone—or some*thing*—collects all that information. To study it. To analyze it. To *digest* it.

And so, consider yourself warned. Next time you scroll through your feed…

It might be feeding on you.

TWO PINOCCHIOS
by Blair Daniels & Craig Groshek

My phone call was interrupted by mewling at the back door.

Meeeeeooooow!, followed by a scratching sound across the glass. It sounded like a cat. Hungry, angry, or both.

"Look, Jim," I said, trying to ignore the sound. "You're going to do fine tomorrow. All you need to remember is that *Michael* started the fight, not you, okay? There were no security cameras, no witnesses. It's your word against his."

Meeeeooooowwww!

"Look, I gotta go, alright? We'll talk tomorrow."

I pocketed my cell phone and made my way to the back door. *Dammit.* Not one — but *two* — stray cats sat on my back porch, little more than silhouettes in the dying sunlight.

I rolled the door open. "Hey! Scram!" I said, shooing them off.

They stared up at me. *Meeeeooooooowww.*

They were nice-looking for cats, I guess. Better-looking than the usual mangy strays I saw on the sidewalk, anyway. One was a gray tabby with bright green eyes; the other was black, with pale blue eyes the color of the sky.

"I said get out of here!" I shouted.

They didn't move.

I sighed and slid the door shut. As soon as it clicked into place, the constant mewling started up again. I popped in earbuds, sat down at my computer, and pulled up my client's case. *Jim Walfort.* Charged with aggravated assault. As long as he kept his story straight tomorrow, he was looking at only a few years at most —

Mreeeeeeeow!

A high-pitched wail broke my thoughts. I turned to see the two cats, still standing on the porch. One was standing on its hind legs, now, pressing its paws against the glass.

"Oh, for Pete's sake." I shoved myself out of the seat and walked over to the door. "Get out of —"

As soon as I yanked the door open, they darted inside.

"Dammit!"

The black cat immediately leapt into my armchair, making itself at home in the soft cushions. The gray one bounded under the table, tail flicking behind it.

Both watched me, perfectly still.

In the inside light, I could tell, now, that they were wearing lengths of twine around their necks. A silver medal dangled from each. *Oh, their owner is going to get an earful.* I stormed over to the black one, on the armchair. I expected it to dart off as I approached; but instead, it stayed perfectly still. Watching.

I turned the tag over in my fingers. I thought I'd find a phone number, or an address; instead, only one word was engraved on the tag.

Auges

"Is that your name? *Auges?*" I bent over and peeked at the gray cat's tag. It read *Kiefer.*

What kind of owner doesn't even put their contact info on the tag?

I stared at the cats. They stared at me. At least they were quiet now.

I would've spent more time getting rid of them, but I had a lot of work to do preparing for tomorrow's case. I put a saucer of milk on the floor, which they both bounded over to. Then I sighed, turned from their prying eyes, and sat back down on the computer.

***

I woke up two hours later in my computer chair. I groaned and rubbed my eyes. 1:06 AM. I'd fallen asleep right at my desk.

I lifted my head and glanced around the living room.

The cats were gone.

My house had a cat door from the previous residents. They must have found it and snuck out. There was no sign that they'd even been here — except for the clumps of gray and black hair shed onto the carpet.

I hauled myself up to the bedroom and slept for another four hours. Then I put on my suit, drove to court, and promptly forgot all about the cats.

"My client, Mr. Walfort, was only acting in self-defense," I said, staring into the judge's blue eyes. "Michael Sheinman attacked my client. He feared for his life, and tried everything to get Mr. Sheinman away from him."

I glanced at the plaintiff. Mr. Sheinman still had the scars running down his face, starkly white against his bronze skin. His attorney sat next to him, her face twisted with concern.

"It's a simple case of self-defense, your honor."

Less than an hour later, we had the verdict. *Not guilty.* "You're amazing, Carlo," Jim whispered to me, as we left the courtroom. "Thank you."

"Of course," I said, patting him on the back.

I left the courtroom feeling great, looking forward to a long weekend.

Until I got home.

I heard them before I even opened the door. *Meow, meeeeooow.* As I stepped in, they both fell silent, staring at me with eyes of blue and green.

Damn cats. Just like people — you give them an inch, they take a yard. Give them a little milk, they come back for more.

"Fine," I muttered. I pulled the fridge door open. Milk sloshed in the bowl. With a clink, I set it down on the tile; the cats came running forward.

My heart stopped.

The cats looked... *different.* Kiefer's snout was slightly scrunched and flattened, as if perpetually snarling. Auges' sky-blue eyes looked too large for its face. The pupils had thinned to vertical slits, despite the dim light.

Something was off about their movements, too. As they leapt for the milk, they didn't do it with all the grace and elegance of a cat. It was more of a limping, off-tempo motion. Like a child just learning to walk.

As their tongues hit the bowl, I jumped back.

What was that smell? Not the musty smell of an animal. No. The smell of fresh-cut pine, as if they'd both spent their day rolling in pine needles. Or potpourri.

A heavy dread settled in my chest. Then I decided to act.

I pulled the bowl out from underneath their noses. "Get *out!*" I shouted. "Out!" They shrieked and mewled in protest. I pulled the door open and chased them out. Then I slid the door closed. Pulled the blinds shut.

Then I pushed the coffee table in front of the cat door.

They wouldn't be coming here anymore.

***

The next week went by without incident.

I didn't see the cats. And thus, I slowly forgot about them. I had more important things to think about — like the Valentino case. It was the first high profile case I'd ever been assigned. I couldn't screw it up.

I met with Mrs. Valentino the evening before the trial.

"He deserved it," she said, in her thick New Jersey accent. "In fact, he deserved worse. First, I should've cut off his —"

"As I've said before, Mrs. Valentino, it's not my business whether you're guilty or not. My only goal is to get you the best sentence possible."

She nodded.

"You should dye your hair, maybe get glasses," I said, looking over her bleach-blonde hair. "We're trying for that meek, motherly type to win the jury over."

"Fair enough," she said, shooting me a crooked grin.

The day of the trial, things went well. The people of the jury were sympathetic to her story — at least, they appeared to be, from their nods and smiles. A few of the women even teared up as she took the stand, and sobbed out a fabricated story of how Mr. Valentino cheated on her on their anniversary.

"Look at her," I said in my closing remarks, gesturing to Mrs. Valentino. "Do you really believe that woman could kill the love of her life? She is a mother, an artist, a woman beloved by her community. The forensics don't mean a thing. Of *course* her fingerprints were all over the crime scene! She was his —"

Mrow.

I stopped. Whipped around. My heart pounded in my chest.

Scrtch, scrtch.

I scanned the courtroom. There — A flash of silver among the wooden seats. *What? There's no way —*

"Mr. Collodi?"

I glanced up at the judge.

"Yes. Sorry." *Come on. Keep it together.* I sighed, and continued: "Your Honor, there simply isn't enough proof to convict this woman. She's inno—"

Mrow.

A black shadow zipped across the floor, behind the jury box.

"Your Honor, uh, I..."

Mrow!

"I conclude my argument."

I sat down. Sweat poured across my brow. The suit felt tight, hot, constricting. I quickly pulled off the jacket, procuring odd looks from the jury.

I arrived home exhausted. The jury was in deliberation, and would be for days, most likely; but after my performance, I had little hope that Mrs. Valentino would end up a free woman. *This was supposed to be your big break. Your high-profile case, to make you a household name,* I told myself.

What would Mom and Dad think?

Angiolina and Domenico. Two Italian immigrants, who owned a tiny restaurant on Maple Ave. They never thought I would get that far.

And maybe, now, I never would.

I walked up the sidewalk and opened the front door.

The strong smell of pine hit me before I even stepped inside.

The cats stood in the kitchen. Waiting for me. Auges in the armchair, tail softly flicking behind it. Kiefer near the back door.

They didn't look like cats anymore.

They were horribly disfigured. Auges' eyes took up half its face. Its nose was elongated and pointed, like a shrew's. Kiefer's face crumpled in on itself. A mess of wrinkled fur that sagged and hung off the bones. Their legs were twice as long as they should have been, bending at unnatural angles when they stepped forward.

And their eyes were no longer green and blue.

They were pure black.

I ran at them. "Get *out!*" I screamed. "Out! Out!"

A chaotic chase ensued. They darted into the kitchen; I grabbed a skillet and waved it at them, hoping to appear a threat. They dashed past me, underneath my legs, into the foyer.

Then they slipped out the cat door, mewling.

How did they get in? I glanced at the overturned coffee table next to the front door. *How did that happen?!* I grabbed a hammer and a box of nails. *Thwack, thwack —* I hammered the cat door shut.

That would keep them out. For good.

***

My sleep was plagued with nightmares.

Of faceless, masked men breaking into my home. As they tied me down and cocked a gun against my head, the cats just watched. Tails flicking. Softly mewling.

Their bottomless black eyes watching as the gun fired into my skull.

I woke up in a cold sweat. Gray dawn shone through the window, and I pulled myself out of bed. When I finally got dressed and left the house, I found the only trace of them — a track of muddy footprints, leading away from the door.

Those were misshapen, too. They looked more like talons than paws.

I hurried to work. Took the elevator up to the top floor. Gormund & Jenkins, Criminal Defense. Nearly tripped on the way to my desk.

"Carlo, are you alright? You look terrible."

Mary Wittel walked over to me, her pretty face twisted with concern.

"Yeah, I'm okay. Just stressed."

"I believe it. That Valentino case... phew. But it's worth it. You already got more media coverage than any other person here." Her eyes lit up. "Say, want to go out tonight? To celebrate?"

"The decision's not out yet."

"I'm sure you crushed it. Meet me at 7, at the Cedar Grill?"

"Uh, sure."

I turned back to my computer. Smiling, for the first time in a while.

7 arrived quickly. Before I knew it, I was sitting at a table outside, watching the flames of the torch dance. At 7:05, she joined me. Red dress, heels, dark hair pulled back in a sleek bun.

This was a date.

I felt the stress slowly melt away.

"So what are your big plans after the Valentino case? Maybe move to New York City, become some hotshot attorney?" she asked, taking a sip of wine.

I shot her a smile. "I think I just might. I've already got some offers from firms up there. Paying double what Gormund & Jenkins does."

"That's great. Yeah, I'm starting to get sick of the firm, too. I'm on the Rivera case and it's a real doozy. So many pieces of confounding evidence and —"

She stopped mid-sentence, her eyes fixed on a point above my shoulder.

"Mary?"

"Look."

I slowly turned around.

The cats.

They stood on the street, peering around a parked SUV. Kiefer no longer had ears; instead there were just holes on the side of its head. Auges's eyes drooped halfway down its face, as if melting in the heat.

Both stayed perfectly still. Watching us.

"No, no, no."

"Carlo?"

I stood up. "We need to move inside. Now."

"What? Why?"

"They keep following me. I can't get rid of them. I don't know what they are, or why they're doing this to me —"

"Carlo," she said. Her voice was soft and steady, as if speaking to a child. "Are you afraid of cats?"

"Those aren't cats," I said, with a scoff. "They're *monsters*. They try to claw their way inside my house every night. They follow me and threaten me. And —"

I turned around. Mary was picking up her purse, heading for the door.

"Wait! Where are you going?"

"I'm leaving," she huffed. "I can't believe I ever asked you out." With a swish of her red dress, she was gone. I was alone.

I turned back around.

The cats were closer, now. Much closer. They sat several feet from the dinner table, watching me. Tails flicking back and forth.

I ran.

I could hear their claws clicking against the cement. Hear their panting breaths, feel their hearts pounding after mine. I ran into the parking lot. I dove inside my car, locked the doors.

Then I began to back up.

Beep beep beep.

I glanced at the rearview camera.

The two cats stood behind the car, their eyes glowing white on the screen. Knobby, emaciated, legs bent at strange angles.

I stomped on the gas.

A sickening bump.

I pulled out of the parking lot without looking back.

I arrived home feeling more relaxed than I had felt in weeks. I took off my shoes, sat back in the armchair, and let my body relax.

A few seconds later, the scratching started.

Scrtch, scrtch. Meeeooooow.

I sprang up and ran to the windows. Peering through the blinds, I saw them there. Standing on my porch, scratching at the cat door, more misshapen than ever.

"I killed you!" I screamed. "How are you still alive?"

Meeeeooow.

"Why are you doing this to me?"

I thought back to the first night I brought them in. When they still looked like cats. Then I defended Jim Walfort. That's when they started to twist and deform, taking on their monstrous appearance.

They changed even more after I defended Mrs. Valentino.

Even more after I lied to Mary about getting lucrative job offers.

Lies. They're after me because of all the lies I've told.

Scrtch. Scrtch. The scratching sound pounded in my ears, but I tried to shut it out. I pulled out my cell phone and dialed the police.

"Westchester Police Department, how can I —"

"I have information on the Valentino case," I blurted. I must've sounded like a madman, panting, shaking, nearly crying. "I need to discuss it with you immediately."

As soon as I spoke, the scratching stopped.

Telling the police everything meant breaking attorney-client privilege. I swiftly lost my law license, and found myself unemployed immediately following. Despite knowing I did the right thing, I quickly spiraled into depression as I spent every day alone in my house, wondering where to go from here.

Seven days later, I heard it.

Meow.

I looked out the window. There the two cats stood. Auges and Kiefer. They looked like cats, now. Fluffy, cute, watching me with their blue and green eyes.

After a moment's hesitation, I opened the door.

They bounded in. I filled a bowl with milk, just like I used to, and set it down on the floor. They lapped it up excitedly.

As I watched them, the thought came to me.

The little restaurant on Maple Ave.

My dad was always looking for hard-working, honest employees. I'd make a quarter the salary I did at Gormund & Jenkins, and the hours would be tough... but at least I wouldn't be lying. Getting guilty people off the hook. Protecting murderers like Mrs. Valentino.

A month later, I was moved out of the house, making the drive across the country back to my hometown.

And that's where I am now. I like it here. The work is harder — no sitting in an air-conditioned office all day, raking in heaps of money — but it's honest work.

As I finished bussing the last table, I heard my dad's voice from behind the counter. "Time to close up," he said, shooting me a smile.

"Just a second." I walked into the kitchen and grabbed the brown paper bag of leftover scraps. I continued out the back door, into the dark alleyway, next to the dumpster. I whistled.

Two cats came bounding out of the darkness. A black cat and a gray tabby.

"Here you go, Auges," I said, placing down a leftover piece of fish. "And Kiefer."

They looked just like they were supposed to. Moss green and sky-blue eyes. Pink noses, cute little paws, fluffy fur.

Just two cats, enjoying the night's leftovers.

I smiled and headed back inside the restaurant.

CELEBRITY

I work for a very high-profile celebrity. I can't tell you who, at the risk of my life.

But I can tell you this: she, as you know her, does not exist.

We come in at 8 AM. The whole committee has never even met her, despite the fact we've worked here four years. Marge claims she glimpsed her once going into our building — but the rest of us don't believe her.

She has better things to do than deal with us.

Social media comes first. Annabelle drafts up a Tweet. Could be anything, but usually it's a down-to-earth joke or vague political commentary. Then, we send it to our focus group. 50 girls, 15-35 in age. That's my job as resident number-cruncher. I analyze the results and decide if it's worthy of posting.

If it isn't, we start over.

If we need it to be personal, we take a photo of Rebecca from behind. She's the only blonde in the group, and is a good stand-in for the real thing. If they want a cute "pet photo," we take a photo of Ben's dogs.

The fans have never noticed.

In fact, every detail of her life that makes it to the public — relationships, feuds, even "scandals" that are "leaked" — are all carefully manufactured and curated. I don't think she's even met up with her "serious boyfriend of three years," other than to get purposefully caught by the paparazzi.

It all went to shit when Marge decided she wanted to meet her.

"I'm going to do it," she told us, grinning ear to ear. "I'm going to meet her."

"How?" Ben asked.

"Why?" I asked.

"Because. I have a theory." She pulled out her phone, tapped a few times. "Look at this photo. From her concert in September. Look at her ears."

"Okay," I said. "What about them?"

"She's got huge earlobes, right? But in *this* photo," she yanked her phone back and swiped a few times, "she's got cute, little, connected earlobes."

All of us stared at her.

"It's not the same person."

"What?" Rebecca asked.

"It's different people! If you take a closer look, the noses are different, too. Just *slightly*. And think about it — it would be easy to turn any skinny, blonde girl into her. What we think of as her 'face' is really just 90% makeup. The dark lipstick, the false eyelashes, all the contouring." As she spoke, Marge's voice became more manic, more frenzied.

"What next, Marge? A tinfoil hat?" Ben asked, arms crossed against his chest.

A few murmured in agreement. She ignored them, and continued, emphatically: "I think it's not just her perception, her persona, that's fake. I think [redacted] doesn't exist."

"Then who sings her songs?" Annabelle asked, through *smacks* of chewing gum.

"Some nameless, faceless employee paid 20 bucks an hour."

"Yeah, but she's met fans," Ben said.

"One of her *doppelgangers* has met fans," Marge corrected.

"But —"

"Look. I'm going to try and meet her, okay? I'm not here so you can talk me out of it." She glanced around the room, a smile on her face. "I'm here to ask who wants to come with me."

"I will."

Marge turned to me and smiled. "11 o'clock tonight, then. My place."

***

The plan was to drive to [redacted]'s address. This wasn't the address that made it into all the magazines, the tabloids; it was the address listed on our paychecks and the organization itself.

We got there in under 20 minutes. It was a country estate, on the outskirts of the city. We parked half a mile down the street. "Wear this," Marge said, passing me a black, wool cap.

That's when reality sunk in.

"We could be arrested for this, couldn't we?"

"Not really. We're not breaking in. We're just taking a look."

My heart pounded as I pulled the hat over my hair.

We slunk out into the darkness, keeping low as we walked along the side of the street. Her mansion loomed into view — white pillars, bay windows. Marble statues peeked through the hedges in the backyard. The quiet splashes of a fountain echoed from somewhere unseen.

No lights were on in the house.

"She's probably out," I said.

"Or she doesn't exist," Marge replied.

We crept around the corner, to the side of the house. That's when we saw one light *was* on, on the second floor. Golden light spilled out into the grass.

"Someone's up there," Marge said.

"Maybe we should get out of here —"

"No. I'm going to see who it is." Marge ran over to a nearby tree. She climbed fast, with more agility than any 45-year-old woman should possess. Then she stretched her neck, and the golden light washed over her face.

Her eyes widened.

"Oh my God."

"Marge?"

She didn't reply.

I climbed up onto one of the rocks. With a deep breath, I jumped.

I only saw it for a second. A flash of the image, like a photograph.

A still, lifeless body lay across a bed. She looked just like *[redacted]*. A man bent over her, holding a knife. The whole scene lit in the soft, golden glow of the lamps.

My heart thundered in my chest. I jumped again.

No. It wasn't a knife.

It was a soldering iron.

And now he was staring straight at us.

I opened my mouth to call to Marge. But it was too late.

CRACK

A shot thundered through the air. From the forest. Marge dropped out of the tree. Her body hit the ground with a sickening *thump.*

Shot right in the forehead.

I ran. I ran as fast as I could, away from the house, down the street. I didn't stop until I got to the car, panting like mad.

I called 911. Even though I knew Marge was beyond saving.

"What is your emergency?"

"My friend was just shot. Please, send someone out here —"

"Where are you now?"

"*[redacted]* Willow Street."

Silence from the other line.

Then her voice cut through the speaker, curt and crisp:

"I'm sorry, we can't find that address."

Click.

I stared in disbelief at my phone.

The next morning, the news said that Marge had committed suicide. Alone in her apartment.

But I know the truth.

THE CHURCH

We found the cathedral on the west side of the city.

It looked out of place. Gothic arches clashed against rectangular high-rises. Gray stone against polished metal. Mullioned windows against mirrored glass. A relic from a different time, standing still as the town around it transformed to a bustling metropolis.

Which cathedral is it?

I looked down at my tourist map. It wasn't marked as an attraction. Even though it looked nicer than half the cathedrals we'd seen so far.

"Want to check it out?" I asked Rose.

"*Another* church? Haven't we seen like five, already?"

"But this one looks so pretty."

She sighed, exasperated. "Fine, fine. As long as we're out by 5:30."

We started across the street. I walked in front of her and pulled open the heavy oak door.

"Woah."

The ceiling stretched far above us, held up by stone columns. The altar was breathtaking, painted in white and gold, flanked by two statues—the Virgin Mary and St. Joseph. Stained glass windows on either side glowed in brilliant blue and gold from the afternoon sun.

I pulled out my phone and took a photo.

"This one's nicer than the other ones we've seen," I said, as we passed the rows of carved pews. "I mean, look at the—"

"Sssssssh."

Rose gestured to the front of the church, and that's when I saw him. A man, kneeling in the rightmost front pew. Head deeply bowed, hands tightly pressed together.

"Oh, I didn't even see him," I whispered. "Sorry."

We walked forward. When we got within a few pews of the man, we made a left, veering away from him. The stone arched elegantly above us, and I lifted my phone to take a few photos.

"Corinne?"

Something about the way she whispered my name made me freeze. She sounded... afraid, all of a sudden.

I walked over to her. She stood in front of the statue of the Virgin Mary, a puzzled look on her face.

"I'm not Catholic, but... that doesn't look like Mary."

I looked up at the statue.

And froze.

The blue-and-white robes looked like Our Lady. As did the flowing brown hair and tan skin. But a strange, white scar ran from her forehead to her chin.

And her face was contorted in anger.

"She's not supposed to look like that. Right?"

"No. That's... really strange."

We walked back towards the center of the church. The front pew was empty, now—the praying man was gone.

I bowed my head as we passed the altar. Then I continued to the other side of the church.

This one had an alcove for candles. To light for prayer intentions. Most churches back in the US have transitioned to electronic candles, but these were real. The statue of St. Joseph stood next to them, carved robes dancing in the flickering light.

I took a step closer—and realized it wasn't St. Joseph at all.

The statue had the same face as the "Mary" one. A scar running from forehead to chin. The same angry expression: eyebrows furled, lip curled, teeth bared.

I stepped back, my heart pounding in my chest, as it glared back at me.

"Let's go," Rose said, tugging at my arm. "This place is kind of giving me the creeps."

I nodded. As we walked back across the altar, though, my gaze caught on a silver bowl. Holy water. "Wait, Rose. Let me get some holy water."

"Really?" she said, with an exasperated sigh.

"I'll just be a second."

"You know, I don't get the whole holy water thing," Rose said as I walked towards the bowl. "Like, what is it supposed to *do?* I get that the wine and the wafers are supposed to be Jesus' blood and body, but the holy water is just... kind of weird."

"Holy water is water blessed by a priest. We use it to—"

My breath caught in my throat.

The bowl wasn't filled with water.

It was filled with blood.

No. It can't be blood. It must just be something... that looks like blood. Rose joined my side, and cupped a hand over her mouth. "Oh, man, what *is* that?"

"I don't know. Wine?"

She looked at me, and I stared back. Both of us unwilling to say out loud what we were thinking. "Let's go," she said, nudging my elbow.

"Yeah."

We walked back up the aisle. As we did, I looked up—and my eyes fell on the stained glass windows. *No.* They didn't depict the seven sacraments, or the saints, or any other Christian scene.

They were covered in strange symbols. Overlapping gold ovals, that reminded me of Celtic knots and pentagrams all at once. And there, in the middle pane, was that same face. The angry expression. The scar that ran across his face, depicted in white, pearlescent glass.

As I stared up at them, someone tugged on my arm. Hard.

I wheeled around. Rose stood behind me, her face white with fear.

"What's wrong?"

She pointed behind us.

A man stood there. Glaring at us.

Judging by the clothes and the haircut, it was the same man we'd seen praying earlier. But now that I saw his face—I recognized him.

It was the scarred, angry face.

The same face on every statue, every window of this church.

I grabbed Rose's hand and we ran. The dark wooden pews, the blue windows, the gray stone—it all whipped by us in a blur of color. The central aisle seemed so much longer, now that fear propelled us instead of awe.

I glanced back.

The man stood in front of the altar, watching us.

We broke out onto the sidewalk. But we didn't stop running until we'd made it several blocks away. Then we called a cab back to our hotel room and spent the rest of the evening there. Too scared to venture back out into the city.

Afraid of what—and who—we might find.

I wish I could tell you that the church didn't exist. That I looked for it later, and couldn't find it. That it had mysteriously blinked off the face of the Earth.

But no—the last day of our trip, I scraped up the courage to walk by it one more time. And it was still there.

Right down to the stone pillars out front, carved with the face of the scarred man.

ICE ROAD TRUCKER

I'm an ice road trucker.

Every winter, I drive my semi up the Dalton Highway in Alaska to deliver supplies. Other drivers complain about how isolated the road is, but I love it. Driving through expanses of snow-covered wilderness, surrounded by nothing by the stars... it's the dream.

Well... it *was* the dream. Until the night of January 17th, 2017.

I was driving the stretch between Coldfoot and the Prudhoe Bay oilfield, around midnight. It's the loneliest part of the highway – 200+ miles with no gas stations, restaurants, no cell phone reception. No traces of civilization at all.

Then my headlights rolled over a truck.

It had skidded off the road and flipped on its side. From the distance, I couldn't tell if it was fresh – or a week-old wreck the recovery crews hadn't picked up yet.

"Hey! Jim!" I yelled.

He was back in the sleeper. We drove together and took turns, so we didn't have to stop for the night. Besides, it was always safer to have a second person if we ran into an emergency.

He poked his blond head out. "What?"

"Look."

The wreck rapidly approached. It was dark – no headlights, no fire, no lights on in the cabin. Just a metal husk breaking the otherwise monotonous Alaskan landscape.

"Poor fella," he said, reaching for the cup in the holster. A long *slurrrp* echoed from behind me. "This road gets mighty nasty sometimes."

"Maybe we should stop. See if they need help."

"Nah. It's an old wreck. Look how dark it is."

Uneasiness settled in my stomach. I'd always felt safe driving up the Dalton highway—because fellow truckers were so helpful. Once, when I'd gotten a flat, no less than three stopped in to make sure I was all right.

It was like we were all part of an unspoken brotherhood, looking out for each other.

I stomped on the brakes. The truck screeched to a halt.

"Hey!" Jim protested. "We're stopping?!"

"Sorry. I need to make sure no one's in there." Leaving the headlights on, I swung the door open, and pulled myself down.

"Wait, wait! I'm comin'!" Jim called after me, pulling on a coat.

I didn't wait for him. Instead, I walked ahead, ice crunching noisily under my boots. The cold wind bit into my exposed face, and I grimaced.

"Hello?" I called out, into the darkness.

No answer.

"Anyone there?" I called again.

"See? No one there," Jim said, coming up behind me. "Stopped for nothin'."

I ignored him and walked towards the cabin. It was facing away from us, pointed towards the forest in the distance.

The trailer was nondescript—no logos or color—but the back hatch was open. Rolled up just a few inches.

Jim called out behind me: "See! They removed all the supplies already, left the hatch open. This thing's probably been here for weeks."

"Okay, I get it," I called back, annoyed. "I just want to check out the cabin, alright? Humor me."

"Humor you! Peh! We're wasting precious time, Danny."

I ignored him and walked across the frozen plain, my boots crunching loudly through the snow. I rounded the corner and came upon the cabin.

I stopped dead in my tracks.

It was a mangled mess of metal. The hood crunched like a tin can. The sideview mirror dangled limply. There was no windshield—just a misshapen hole, where it used to be.

Through it, I could make out the driver's seat. It was horribly buckled and bent, conjuring awful images of what the driver must have looked like.

"Hello?" I called through the window. It looked empty, but just in case.

All was silent.

"It's empty, huh?" Jim asked, a wild smile on his face.

"Yeah. And I don't think the driver made it," I replied, my mouth suddenly dry.

"The highway, she takes 'em good, sometimes. Nothin' we can do. Just the circle of life and all that."

Great. Jim was waxing poetic, now. "Okay, Jim," I said, cutting him off. "Let's get back on the road."

That's when I noticed it.

The snow around the truck was undisturbed. No swirl of frantic footprints from the rescue team. No tire tracks from police cars racing to the scene. No grooves from the body being dragged away.

The cabin was empty... the driver had most likely perished... and no rescue team had come out?

"Why aren't there any prints around here?" I asked Jim. "If the rescue team came out..."

"Must be weeks old, as I said. Pro'lly snowed ten times since they got him and the supplies out. Covered the prints right up."

"I guess you're right." That did make sense. Now that I took a closer look, there weren't any skid marks in the snow from the truck, either. Defeated, I turned and walked back towards our truck.

"Wait — what's *this?*"

I turned around. Jim was crouched in the snow, trailing a finger across the ground.

"What's what?"

"These *prints!*"

I walked back over and crouched beside him.

There were several overlapping trails of footprints. They began at the back door of the trailer, weaved through the snow, and ended somewhere in the darkness of the plains. And they looked *fresh*. The edges were sharp and clean, not softened by the wind or snowfall.

"That doesn't make any sense. We're in the middle of nowhere. Not a single soul for miles around."

"Then who made these prints?"

"I don't know..."

"Let's find out." Jim walked over to the back door, and with a grunt, pulled it open.

Schhliiiip.

The metallic sound reverberated through the trailer, echoing against the snow. I pulled a flashlight from my pocket and flicked it on.

"What the hell?"

The trailer looked... *lived* in.

Empty glass bottles glinted in the light, stacked up in a line against the wall. Clothing was strewn everywhere. In the right corner, they were piled up with a blanket to form a rough bed.

"There's nobody for two-hundred miles, at least," he said with fascination, pulling himself up into the trailer. "What the heck is going on here?"

"Hey, wait," I called after him. "We shouldn't—"

"Tools back here, Danny," he called out, his voice echoing in the metal box. "All kinds of knives and spears and stuff. I s'pose that's how he gets his food. Hunts it down."

I stepped onto the lip of the trailer and hoisted myself inside. The air was musty, damp, and cold—though warmer than the outside. The floor, which was really the side of the trailer, was tilted at a slight angle.

I glanced around. While there were many household items I recognized—knives, shears, clothes—there were some I didn't. A black medallion, emblazoned with a strange symbol next to the 'bed' area. A stone bowl and stick that resembled a mortar-and-pestle.

"Danny, take a look at this."

I turned the flashlight towards him—and jumped back.

White bone. Twisted mouths. Sunken eye sockets.

More than a dozen animal skulls, all lined up in a neat row at the back wall. The first was tiny—the size of a mouse head. They grew progressively larger, the last ones looking like they belonged to deer, caribou, moose.

And painted on the ground, under our feet... was some sort of symbol. A circle with strange characters all around it. Like letters from an unknown language.

"This is freakin' creepy," Jim said. "Wish I brought my camera."

Despite my thick jacket, a chill went up my spine. "Come on, Jim. Let's go. Like you said, we're wasting time. We'll get to Prudhoe late, and—"

"Oh, *now* you care about wasting time?" His blue eyes met mine. "You're just a scaredy-cat, that's what you—"

Thunk.

We both froze.

The sound had been faint. But in the absolute silence of this Alaskan wasteland, it was more than just a random sound. More than the wind, the forest, the Earth could produce.

"You hear that?" Jim whispered.

We listened, but there was only silence.

"Okay. Let's get outta here." Jim said, taking a step forward.

We walked to the front of the trailer, our footsteps shaking the metal. Then we jumped down, into the snow.

My blood ran cold.

A man stood in the darkness.

Dressed head-to-toe in black, tattered clothing. A hood veiled his face in shadow. And a knife glinted in his right hand, catching the light of our headlights.

We broke into a run.

He bolted forward. Crunching footsteps rang out behind us. Growing louder by the second. My lungs burned in the cold air, but I forced myself forward.

My hand fell on the metal handle of the truck.

I dove in. Jim followed me a second later. *Click, click, click*—he madly pressed the *lock* button. I turned the key, and the engine rumbled underneath us.

"Drive!" Jim yelled, panting.

My headlights flashed over the man. He stood still in the snow, staring at us with wild, blue eyes. Gripping the knife tightly.

And behind him... more figures materialized around the fallen trailer. All wearing black, hooded clothing. They remained still, their heads turning to stare as we pulled onto the highway.

Then they were left in the dust, as we sped forward into the Alaskan wilderness.

***

We called the police—but by the time they made it out there, the truck had been cleaned up. It was just an empty old wreck. No animal skulls, no strange symbols, no sign that anyone ever lived there.

I haven't driven a truck up the Dalton highway since that night. I still deliver supplies, but to other parts of Alaska. Never again will I voluntarily drive up that cursed road.

But, sometimes, I hear about disappearances along that highway. A lonely trucker, here or there, vanishing into thin air. His vehicle left behind, parked on the side of the road.

And I know he didn't just get lost on that lonely stretch of highway.

He was *taken*.

EXCELLENT CUSTOMER SERVICE

The following correspondence was found on a defunct computer sold during the bankruptcy of the children's toy manufacturer ToysEveryday™.

From: "Elizabeth Harmin" <e.harmin@xxxxx>
To: "ToysEveryday Customer Service" <help@toyseveryday.com>

Dear ToysEveryday,

I am VERY dissatisfied with our Ally Bally doll.

You clearly say on the website that she will say "I love you, Mommy!" every time her hand is squeezed. THIS DOES NOT HAPPEN. Every time we squeeze her hand, she says "Mommy will be gone soon." It is scaring my daughter. This was one of her only Christmas presents and now Christmas is RUINED.

If you don't send us a replacement I am going to leave a VERY bad review on your website.

Beth Harmin

—-

From: "ToysEveryday Customer Service" <help@toyseveryday.com>
To: "Elizabeth Harmin" <e.harmin@xxxxx>

Dear Beth,

Thank you for contacting ToysEveryday™ Customer Service! We'd be happy to assist you with your recent inquiry.

We have shipped a new Ally Bally™ doll to your home. However, it is of the utmost importance that you dispose of your current doll in the proper way. We want you to have a safe, fun, and happy experience with our products!

Please follow these instructions exactly:

1. Using twine, fishing line, or another strong variety of string, tie the doll's hands together and wrap her up in the string. This is

just to ensure no small pieces get loose!

2. Using a match or lighter, light your Ally Bally™ doll on a fire. Let her burn for no less than one (1) hour. For safety, you may find it easiest to place her in a fire pit, fireplace, or other receptacle.

3. Dispose of the ashes and burnt pieces in a body of water, e.g. a lake, an ocean, etc. Do NOT use a pond, as this is too small.

4. Enjoy your replacement doll!

Thank you so much for contacting ToysEveryday™ Customer Service! We're happy to assist you. Please consider taking a brief survey to let us know how we've helped you, by clicking here.

Thank you,

Shauna
ToysEveryday Customer Service

—-

From: "Elizabeth Harmin" <e.harmin@xxxxx>
To: "ToysEveryday Customer Service" <help@toyseveryday.com>

Are you really asking me to SET THE DOLL ON FIRE??? We don't even have a fireplace! What is this? Can't I just send the old doll back to you?

—-

From: "ToysEveryday Customer Service" <help@toyseveryday.com>
To: "Elizabeth Harmin" <e.harmin@xxxxx>

Dear Beth,

Yes, you may send the old doll back to us, but you have to pay return shipping.

—-

From: "Elizabeth Harmin" <e.harmin@xxxxx>
To: "ToysEveryday Customer Service" <help@toyseveryday.com>

Okay. I burned the doll outside. The fire extinguished after thirty minutes or so, though, and I couldn't get it lit again.

—-

From: "Elizabeth Harmin" <e.harmin@xxxxx>
To: "ToysEveryday Customer Service" <help@toyseveryday.com>

Okay. What kind of business are you running here? We all woke up at 2 AM to the dog barking. Went downstairs to find that damned doll pressed against the window. Half burnt up, still tied up in the string.

My daughter is TERRIFIED. As I type this, she is STILL crying. She has so many questions I can't answer.

We left the doll in the woods behind our house after burning it. How did it get all the way there? Do you have some sort of electronics in it or something? Is that why I was supposed to throw it in water?

Please advise.

Beth

—-

From: "ToysEveryday Customer Service" <help@toyseveryday.com>
To: "Elizabeth Harmin" <e.harmin@xxxxx>

Dear Beth,

You MUST burn your Ally Bally™ doll for no less than one hour. If you stop halfway, the process is incomplete.

Your replacement arrives tomorrow.

Shauna

—-

From: "Elizabeth Harmin" <c.harmin@xxxxx>
To: **"ToysEveryday** **Customer** **Service"** <help@toyseveryday.com>

Shauna,

We got home from work to find your package, with the new doll, shredded to pieces on our doorstep. Like a dog or some animal got into it. The new doll has been decapitated.

Thank God we saw it before our daughter did.

Would you be willing to send another replacement?

—-

From: **"ToysEveryday** **Customer** **Service"** <help@toyseveryday.com>
To: "Elizabeth Harmin" <e.harmin@xxxxx>

Dear Beth,

We have sent another replacement, but you MUST dispose of the original doll properly.

Please tie her in twine, burn her for one (1) hour, and dispose of the remains in a large body of water.

—-

From: "Elizabeth Harmin" <e.harmin@xxxxx>
To: "ToysEveryday Customer Service" <help@toyseveryday.com>

We don't know where doll is.

—-

From: "ToysEveryday Customer Service" <help@toyseveryday.com>
To: "Elizabeth Harmin" <e.harmin@xxxxx>

Dear Beth,

Find her immediately.

—-

From: "Elizabeth Harmin" <e.harmin@xxxxx>
To: "ToysEveryday Customer Service" <help@toyseveryday.com>

Shauna—

After an hour of searching, we have found the original doll. IT WAS IN MY DAUGHTER'S CLOSET.

My daughter claims she didn't do it. I believe her. The sight of the burnt doll alone seems to terrify her. I don't think she's even willing to touch it.

After she goes to sleep tonight, we will complete the steps.

Beth

—-

From: "Elizabeth Harmin" <e.harmin@xxxxx>
To: "ToysEveryday   Customer   Service" <help@toyseveryday.com>

It is done.

—-

From: "Elizabeth Harmin" <e.harmin@xxxxx>
To: "ToysEveryday   Customer   Service" <help@toyseveryday.com>

IloveyouMommyIloveyouMommyIloveyouMommy

—-

From: "Elizabeth Harmin" <e.harmin@xxxxx>
To: "ToysEveryday Customer Service" <help@toyseveryday.com>

WHAT THE HELL? I didn't send that last message, Shauna.

—-

From: "Elizabeth Harmin" <e.harmin@xxxxx>
To: "ToysEveryday Customer Service" <help@toyseveryday.com>

IloveyouMommyIliveyouMommy
IliveyuoMomyAliveyuoMory
AlivenuoMorreAlivenoMore

—-

From: "Elizabeth Harmin" <e.harmin@xxxxx>
To: "ToysEveryday Customer Service" <help@toyseveryday.com>

SHE'S IN OUR BED. IN OUR FUCKING BED, SHAUNA. FACE ALL BURNT AND SCORCHED. EYES GONE.

—-

From: "Elizabeth Harmin" <e.harmin@xxxxx>
To: "ToysEveryday Customer Service" <help@toyseveryday.com>

Alive no More
Alive no More
Alive no More

—-

From: "ToysEveryday Customer Service" <help@toyseveryday.com>
To: "Elizabeth Harmin" <e.harmin@xxxxx>

Dear Beth,

PLEASE EVACUATE YOUR HOUSE IMMEDIATELY. We have notified the relevant authorities.

DO NOT BRING THE DOLL OR HER REPLACEMENT WITH YOU.

Shauna

—-

From: "Elizabeth Harmin" <e.harmin@xxxxx>

To: "ToysEveryday Customer Service" <help@toyseveryday.com>

IloveyouSHAUNAIloveyouSHAUNAIloveyouSHAUNA

—-

From: "Elizabeth Harmin" <e.harmin@xxxxx>
To: "ToysEveryday Customer Service" <help@toyseveryday.com>

We're in the car, driving to my husband's parents Milwaukee. I checked the car five times. No dolls are in here. I didn't even let our daughter take her Barbie doll.

—-

From: "ToysEveryday Customer Service" <help@toyseveryday.com>
To: "Elizabeth Harmin" <e.harmin@xxxxx>

Dear Beth,

We have arrived at your house and are securing the property. Plan to stay with your in-laws for at least two weeks.

Shauna

—-

From: "ToysEveryday Customer Service" <help@toyseveryday.com>
To: "Elizabeth Harmin" <e.harmin@xxxxx>

ALIVE NO MORE
NO MORE ALIVE
NO MORE AL!V3
N0 M0R3 A#!V3
&0 $0R3 4#!^3
@0 %0)3
4#!^3

—-

From: "ToysEveryday Customer Service" <help@toyseveryday.com>
To: "Elizabeth Harmin" <e.harmin@xxxxx>

Dear Beth,

We regret to inform you that during our recovery mission, the house caught fire. I'm terribly sorry. By the time the fire department arrived, it had burned to the ground. There is nothing left.

We have disposed of the doll and her replacements.

This is the last correspondence you will receive from us. Have a nice day.

Shauna
ToysEveryday Customer Service

—-

From: "Elizabeth Harmin" <e.harmin@xxxxx>
To: "ToysEveryday Customer Service" <help@toyseveryday.com>

YOU BURNED DOWN MY HOUSE?!

—-

From: "MAILER-DAEMON" <mailer-daemon@xxxxx>
To: "Elizabeth Harmin" <e.harmin@xxxxx>

Delivery failed: the recipient is no longer at this address.

THE BEAR

"I saw someone in the window."

Dave stood in the backyard, staring up at the dark windows.

Amy turned to me. "I *thought* I told you not to let him watch any scary movies."

"He's an adult. It's not my job to tell him what to do," I replied with a grunt, as I wedged the crowbar between the door and the frame.

"It is, when he's compromising the whole operation. What if he starts screaming because he thinks he saw some little ghostie in the window? The police'll be here in seconds." She glared at me. "If you can't get your little brother to behave, we're not taking him next time."

"Okay, fine. Next time I'll try." I groaned as I pushed the crowbar. *Crack!* The resistance suddenly gave way, and the back door swung open — revealing inky darkness.

Contrary to what you believe, we weren't robbing the place.

We were doing something far dumber.

Dave, Amy, and I run a blog on abandoned places. It usually doesn't involve breaking the law, but this time it was worth it. We'd been asked by the locals to cover the Blue Mansion of Maple Ave.

It was something of a local legend.

The O'Maras were evicted in 2009, after the housing crash and a grueling foreclosure. I'm not going to lie — it made me chuckle a bit, when I heard. Bryan O'Mara was a cruel bully, and his parents had bought the house just to show off. It's stood empty since then, in a strange state of limbo: too decrepit for any investor to buy, but also too "historic" to be demolished. The structure was built in the 1850s — a genuine antebellum mansion.

Keeping this junk around all for "history." I looked up at the house, frowning. The structure was almost entirely subsumed by the surrounding foliage. Saplings grew from the crumbling foundation. Thick vines slithered up the massive white columns. Tangled branches engulfed the porch, completely blocking the front door.

Nature wasted no time in reclaiming her land.

"Dave!" Amy called, as we stood in the doorway. "Come on!"

"But – but what if there's someone in there?" he replied, his voice barely audible from the outside.

"There's no one in here but rats and bugs!"

"I'm not sure that helps," I muttered.

After waiting for Dave to change his mind, we decided to go on without him. I went in first. The white flashlight swept over the floor of the dining room. Dust motes kicked up in the air, catching in the light like glitter.

Snap. The flash of white from Amy's camera threw the room into stark relief. The dining table, still standing against the window. A small painting of the countryside, hanging askew. If it weren't for the dust, blanketing the room like snow, I could've believed the O'Maras moved out yesterday.

"Smaller than I remember," I said.

"You've been here before?"

"I've lived in this town my whole life." I kicked a piece of gravel across the wooden floor. It skittered into the darkness. "*Everyone* knew the O'Maras."

"That's so cool! Were you friends with them?"

I didn't reply.

My eyes had fallen on the staircase.

A pang of fear hit me. I went up there once, with Bryan. I thought he was bringing me to his room to play Guitar Hero. Instead... he showed me his father's taxidermy room.

It was just another way for Mr. O'Mara to show off. The entire room was dedicated to his hunting trophies. Four deer heads – all of them at least eight-point bucks — mounted on the wall. Two turkeys, their necks bright red. And one black bear — reared up on its hind legs, staring straight at me.

Are they still here?

"Let's check out the upstairs," Amy said, walking towards the hallway.

"No. Wait."

"Why?"

"I'm... I'm just not sure that's the best idea."

I was so naive. Even at eight years old, I should have known better. But no — I just strode in there, babbling on about Pokemon.

Then the door slammed shut behind me.

I spent the first twenty minutes screaming at him to open up. A few times, I heard the light thump of a footstep, the creak of a floorboard — but he never came. It was just me and those horrible animals. Stuffed. Dead. Empty. Staring at me with their dark, glass eyes.

Mr. O'Mara found me when he got home from work. Three hours later. After the sun had set, and I'd been in the dark with those things, all alone.

He didn't apologize. He didn't reprimand his son.

He *bribed* me.

I didn't understand what was going on, at the time. All I knew was — he was pushing the Guitar Hero guitar in my hands, telling me everything was okay. "That's a shoddy door. Sometimes locks all by itself. And then Bryan fell down the stairs... what an awful thing to happen. He never even heard you. But don't worry. Everything's fine now. And this is an early birthday present, from the two of us."

I just nodded. Then I spent the rest of the day holed up in my room, playing Guitar Hero. Trying to play the memories away.

"Adam?" Amy called, as she slung the camera around her neck. "Come on."

I hesitated.

"Dave's getting to you, huh?"

"What? No!"

Amy smiled mischievously. She was using my greatest weakness against me, and she knew it. I never liked to look like a coward — *especially* in front of a woman.

Besides, Mr. O'Mara must've taken the animals with him when he was evicted. *Right?*

"Let's go."

I led her out of the dining room. A few broken bottles glinted in the light, sparkling like gems in a mine. I started to climb the stairs — then froze.

Under the shards of glass was a long scratch in the wood.

I took a deep breath and continued to climb the stairs.

With every step, the air grew heavier. Mustier. The sweet smell of summer grass left, leaving only dust and rot. Amy turned left. I followed her, a lump forming in my throat.

There were only two rooms on this side — the master bedroom, and the taxidermy room. Amy reached for the latter first. Turned the knob. I shut my eyes, but that only made it worse. Images flashed through my mind — matted fur. Yellowed fangs. Black, glass eyes.

"Holy shit."

I forced my eyes open.

The deer heads watched us from the wall — antlers caked with dust, black eyes glinting like tiny beetles in the light. Two turkeys huddled in the corner. One had fallen over, laying still across the floor, as if somehow more dead than the others.

"This is incredible!" Amy took out her camera. White light flashed across the room like lightning. *Snap, snap, snap.* "Our readers are going to *freak.* Seriously. Amazing."

I shook my head, staring at the empty space in the center. "No. The bear's gone."

"What?"

"There was a bear. In this room." As I spoke, my skin grew hot. My throat parched. "A black bear, on its hind legs. I remember it."

I wish I could forget...

She lowered the camera, and we were again plunged in darkness. "Seriously? We should find it! Unless you think they took it with them. Aw, man, I hope they didn't —"

Thump.

"What was that?" I whispered.

"Dave, probably. Finally grew a pair and decided to join us."

Thump.

It was heavier, this time. Louder. The sound echoed up the stairs, reverberating through the room. Dust stirred up on the floor in swirling eddies. The disembodied deer heads seemed to widen their eyes with fear.

"Dave does *not* sound like that."

"Who do *you* think it is, then?"

But I couldn't reply. My throat was too dry. My heart throbbed in my chest. The darkness swirled and shifted around me. I lurched forward.

Amy caught me. "Adam? Adam, are you okay?"

I pushed her away and ran out of the room.

The hallway tilted and lurched before me, as if we were at sea. I ran away from the stairs, into the master bedroom. Fumbled with the lock until it clicked into place. As I stood in the darkness, leaned against the wall, the memories came flooding back.

Sitting against the door. Waiting for Bryan to come back. Crying. Sobbing. Screaming. And after the sun went down, the darkness settled in... I could swear it was moving. That they *all* were moving. Every time I opened my eyes, they seemed an inch closer. When Mr. O'Mara finally rescued me from the room, I could've sworn it was just a few feet away from me. Mouth open. Lips curled back. Watching me with those dark, fiery eyes.

But it didn't finish me off then. Even when I knew death was certain, it waited. It knew this moment was coming. Why kill me in an instant, when it could torment me for a decade first?

Thump. The footsteps were closer, now. Coming from the hallway.

They didn't sound so heavy, anymore. They almost sounded... human.

Enough of this. Heart pounding, I pulled out my phone to call 9-1-1. But it was already lit up with a text from Dave, five minutes ago:

I saw it in the window. Get out of there.

My heart stopped.

We'd left Dave in the backyard, when we broke in through the back door. The taxidermy room didn't face the backyard.

The master bedroom did.

I heard muffled shouts from the other side. Amy's voice — and Dave's. I fumbled and slipped against the lock. My hands were too sweaty. Or it was stuck.

A low growl echoed behind me.

"Help!" I shouted. I pounded against the door, frantically. Just like I had over a decade ago. Hot tears ran down my cheeks. "Help me! Please!"

"We're trying!" Amy's voice came through the wood, along with muddied syllables from Dave. The doorknob turned underneath my fingers. The door shook.

It didn't open.

"Help!" I screamed.

Click, click, click. The distinct sound of claws against wood filled the room. The floor shook under my feet.

I turned around.

The faint light from the moon outlined its hulking silhouette. It slowly stalked across the room, toward me, until I could smell its rotten, fetid odor. Hear its tongue race across its lips. Feel its hot breath against my face.

I screamed.

The door snapped open behind me.

Amy wrapped her arms around me, and yanked me out into the hallway. Dave shined the flashlight into the room.

It illuminated a taxidermied black bear.

Perfectly still. Perfectly dead.

"Shhh, it's okay," Amy whispered in my ear. "We're going to leave now, okay?"

"So that's what I saw," Dave said, with a laugh. He walked right up to the bear and shined his light over it. Even from my distance, on the floor of the hallway, I could see how fake the thing looked. Black fur, matted with dust. Glass eyes — maybe even plastic. Yellow, wooden teeth. "It's actually kind of cool."

"Are you okay, Adam?"

I let out a shuddering breath. "Yeah. Sorry. I just... freaked out for a second." I pulled myself up, brushed my pants off. *So much for not looking like a coward.*

She pulled me into a hug.

Then we descended the stairs, piled into the car, and left. As we drove up the gravel driveway, I watched the mansion recede into the distance. The vines that crawled up the columns would soon grow into the windows, the floors. Nature would fill the entire house, reclaiming its territory.

The animals would be back where they belonged.

OPEN HOUSE

I've been house-hunting for two years.

It's absolute torture. Every day, I go online and comb through the listings. Every time I click on a house I like, there's something wrong with it. I check out the satellite image and—*bam!*—it's next to a railroad. Or a sewage treatment plant. Or I scroll down to the details, and the property tax is half my salary. Or the description has those three awful little words: "House sold as-is."

Translation: there is something very, very wrong with this house.

So when I saw a beautiful, 2500-square-foot house for $250K, I was thrilled. Honestly, I didn't even check out the other photos. When I saw the attractive bay windows and brick façade, I was sold.

"I found *the* house!" I squealed, running out to hug Dan.

"You say that every week," he grumbled.

"No, seriously, I found it! It's incredible! And there's an open house tomorrow!"

We drove over to 15 Watcher Lane the next day. As we turned into the long, gravel driveway, Dan frowned. "Are you sure the open house is today?"

There weren't any "FOR SALE" signs or yellow balloons. And as we neared the house, I realized there were no cars in the driveway, either.

The house also looked like it had aged quite a bit since the photographs on Trulia were taken. The paint was flaking. Scrubby weeds poked through the sidewalk. A few shingles were missing from the roof.

It reminded me of going on a date with a guy from an online dating site. He looks *so* handsome in the photo, but when you meet him he's ten years older and bald.

I pulled out my phone. "Nope, the open house is definitely today. One to three PM."

We pulled up to the garage and parked. Dan got out of the car first, tentatively walking down the sidewalk as if it'd burn him. I followed, pulling on my red coat. I noticed the door was missing the lockbox that most for-sale properties have.

Dan knocked, several times.

No one answered.

"Maybe they scheduled it, and then just forgot," he said.

I glanced around the property. It was nearly invisible from the road; large shrubs dotted the edge of the front yard. When we first pulled up, I thought they were a nice privacy feature. Now, however—standing here alone, on the doorstep of an empty house—they seemed foreboding.

Like they were meant to conceal.

"Hey! It's open," Dan said. I turned around—he'd pushed the front door open a few inches. Inside, the house was dark and shadowy.

"Oh, no. We can't just *go in*."

"We drove almost an hour to get here. Might as well take a look around. It *is* supposed to be an open house." He stepped inside; the wood creaked in protest.

Click.

We both froze.

It came from inside the house. And sounded like the shutter of a camera. Or, more accurately, the skeuomorphic shutter sound that a phone makes when you take a picture.

"Let's get out of here."

We ran to the car. As soon as we were inside, I pressed the locks. We pulled back down the gravel driveway, my heart pounding in my chest.

I took one last look at the house before we reached the main road.

There was a flutter of motion in the downstairs window.

"Dan?" I said, my voice trembling. "I... I think there's someone in there."

We both stared as a figure—tall and thin, barely more than a silhouette behind the glass—pulled the curtains shut.

With a screech of tires, he pulled out onto the main road. The house disappeared behind the row of shrubs.

***

Later that night, I was scrolling through the listings again. After clicking on a few more ugly houses, I pulled the tab back up for the house we'd visited. "Hey, Dan! Want to check out the inside of 15 Watcher with me?"

He laughed, uneasily. "You're still interested in it?"

"Maybe."

He joined me on the sofa. I clicked on the first image. Up came a photo of the dining room. A dark cherry wood table, with chairs lined up around it, and the bay window beyond.

"Wait."

At the very edge of the bay window, I saw something. A bit of red. Barely poking into the window's view.

The same color as my jacket.

Heart pounding, I clicked to the next photo.

It was also a photo of the dining room. But this time, out the window, there were two people standing on the sidewalk. A woman in a red coat. A man in a black hoodie.

"That's... that's *us*," I said.

I clicked to the next photo.

It was a photo of the foyer. The front door hung halfway open, and I could see Dan stepping inside. And—behind him—the back of my head.

I clicked to the next one.

The door was closed. Through the window, I could see a blur of red and black, as Dan and I hurried away. But at the very bottom of the photo, there was something.

Something pointed and silver.

The edge of a knife.

SIREN SONG

by Blair Daniels & Craig Groshek

I woke up at 3 AM to someone singing outside my window.

Her voice sounded so close—just inches from my open window. But when I peered out, I didn't see anyone there.

"Hello?" I called out into the night.

No reply.

It was kind of ironic that someone was *singing.* I'm a songwriter, and the last thing you want to hear after a long day of writing is more music. As I started to close the window, I caught a few of the words. Something about 'the true heart underneath.' Sung in a haunting minor key.

I climbed back in bed. When I woke up two hours later, I drank no less than three cups of coffee and sat down at my desk to write.

Unlike the day before, the words came easily to me, somehow jump-started by the eerie song. I began singing to myself:

You waited all those years
Underneath the stones and tears
All alone, cold and still
Until the day we find you well

My pen scratched across the page. The lyrics came fast and swift to me, flowing out like blood. In just a few hours, I'd recorded the entire song, and uploaded it to my channel with the name "Underneath."

The views, and comments, poured in at an astonishing rate. "Best song I've heard in years. You got tons of talent" wrote one user. Another said "this song reminds me so much of some of my darkest days, but in a good way. Great song." As I scrolled through, my pride swelling, I came upon a comment unlike the others:

Haveh ex turnet escution klanchet

What was that? Latin? It wasn't any language I recognized. I would've thought nothing of it, but then my eye caught on the user's name. **Savannahgirl125.** That was one of my "fans" — she commented on every single one of my videos. Nice, typical stuff. Telling me I was super talented, I should release an album, and the like.

She'd never made a weird comment like this one.

I shrugged and closed my laptop. *Maybe her cat walked across the keyboard,* I told myself. Of course, that made no sense; the comment wasn't random. It had spaces and "words," even if they were nonsensical words.

But I didn't think any more of it. Instead, I walked out the door to run some errands.

***

When I got back an hour later and checked the video, I couldn't believe it. The video had almost eighty-thousand views. In just a few hours.

My excitement, however, was quickly deflated by the comments.

There were more like Savannahgirl's. *Dozens* of them. All saying nonsense words. Some of them repeated the words in hers — I saw "haveh" quite a few times. Most were just single sentences, but some were whole paragraphs of nonsense, filling up the screen.

I copied some of the words and pasted them into a translation site. But when I clicked submit, the site said: **no language found.**

Riiiiing.

My thoughs were interrupted by my agent, Dan. "Violet! I saw your video, Underneath. It is *blowing up!* Someone wants to buy the rights to it. Someone *big.* Are you ready? It's —"

"Have you looked at the comments?"

"No. Why?"

I sighed and paced the room, eyeing the laptop with fear. "There are these weird comments, all over the place. They look like they're in a different language, or something."

"Trolls, then."

"No, I mean... *dozens* of people are posting them, Dan. It's about half of all the comments on the video. And other people are replying to them, with more nonsense language."

"Okay, well, that doesn't matter. You need to meet me for lunch so we can go over this deal. Okay?"

"Uh, sure. Okay."

I walked into the cafe with a heavy heart. As an artist, you want to interact with your fans. As a *female* artist, it gets scary sometimes, with all the creeps out there. What if someone was *trying* to scare me? What if a group of my fans had banded together for the sole purpose of freaking me out?

"Violet?"

I turned around — and froze.

Dan was sitting at one of the booths by the window. He was smiling and waving, dressed in his usual gray T-shirt and ripped jeans.

But there was something behind him.

A dark, blurry shadow. It started at his shoulder and grew up towards his head, dissipating into the air as if it were a cloud of smoke. But as he moved — as he bobbed his head, waved his hand — it moved with him.

I sat down across from him.

"What's behind you?"

Dan glanced back, then turned towards me. "Nothing."

"No. There's something behind you. Like smoke. Or a shadow."

"I don't know what you're talking about."

"There's something behind you. There's something —"

I stopped.

It was gone. Dan was staring at me, a concerned look on his face. The area behind him was perfectly clear and bright. No smoke. No shadow. No darkness.

"Nevermind," I muttered. It must've been a trick of the light. Or my imagination. I *was* sleep-deprived, after all. Too much work. Too much coffee.

"Okay. Can I *finally* tell you who wants to buy the song?"

"Sure."

"Chained Up!" he squealed.

"Oh, wow."

"Come on! Show more excitement! They're big in certain circles. This could be our big break."

"I guess."

"So what do you say?"

Finally, a glimmer of excitement spread through me. *This could be my big break. The chance of a lifetime. My song... being heard by millions of people.*

"Okay."

After I signed some paperwork Dan had printed off, I went home, turned on the TV, and promptly fell asleep on the sofa.

***

"A strange incident occurred just outside of Springfield this afternoon."

My eyes fluttered open. I turned towards the TV.

"While driving home from work, motorist Jeff Olsen saw a woman on the side of the road. He's here to tell us the story."

A pale, middle-aged man flashed onscreen.

"I was drivin' home from work when I saw an old woman, just sittin' in the yard behind the Catholic church. St. Monica's, I think it's called. Anyway, I pulled over, got out of my car, and went over to her. I thought she might be, I dunno, hurt or somethin'. I called out to her, asked her if she needed help. She didn't say anything, so I walked right up to her."

"As I got closer, I realized she was diggin'. Just diggin' in the dirt with her bare hands. And the expression on her face... totally blank. Not lookin' at me no matter how much I tried to get her attention. Just staring into space. So finally, I tapped her on the shoulder."

"She turned 'round and grabbed me by the arm. Then she lunged at me and bit me, real hard, right here."

The man held his right arm up. It was swaddled in bandages.

"I ran back towards the car. The woman... she started to chase me. Man, I haven't seen anythin' like it before. Was real mad. Rabid, almost. All the while, shoutin' somethin' in a different language. Somethin' I couldn't understand. But I got in my car, and I —"

I turned the TV off.

Shouting something in a different language. Like the comments on my song? Like **haveh** and those other weird words, that even the translator couldn't pick up?

No. It had to be a coincidence.

That night, I couldn't fall asleep. I went online and checked my video again, which was now up to over half a million views. As I scrolled through the comments, I noticed that *most* of them—at least two-thirds—were in the same strange, nonsensical language as the others.

At 3 AM, I decided to take a drive to calm my nerves.

It was a freezing cold night. I drove down the small-town roads, watching the shops and trees roll by. Everything was closed, at this hour, save for the QuickChek on the corner of Maple Ave. and Main Street.

I'd get a snack there, then try to get some more sleep.

I turned the radio on and scrolled through the stations. Some pop hit. A high tempo dance number. Some song in French. I pressed the seek button over and over.

Until I heard my own voice.

You waited all those years
Underneath the stones and tears
All alone, cold and still
Until the day we find you well

"No, no, no," I muttered. "They stole my song. They stole it!" In my anger, I sped right past the QuickChek and continued down Main Street. My headlights flashed over the General Store, the pharmacy... and then St. Monica's.

I froze.

Several people were standing there.

Standing there in the dark, at 3 AM, in the patch of grass between the church and the cemetery. Only wearing pajamas, not coats, despite the freezing cold. Some of them were digging; others were just standing there, blankly staring at the side of the church. As my headlights rolled over them, they didn't even turn towards me.

As I got closer, I heard the chanting.

I could hear it clearly through the car windows. **Haveh ex turnet escution. Haveh ex turnet escution...**

I pulled out my cell phone. I needed to talk to Dan. I needed to tell him what was happening. How it was all, somehow, seemed to be related to my song.

The song I just sold to an incredibly popular band.

I dialed Dan's number. It rang once. Then, a few seconds later, a familiar noise came through the window.

Dan's Metallica ringtone.

I looked up. There he was, standing near the edge of the crowd. I pulled over the side of the road and leapt out of the car. "Dan!" I yelled. "Dan!"

He turned towards me, face still blank. Then, slowly, the rest of them turned to look at me.

I turned around and ran back to my car. Then I drove home as fast as I could.

***

"Dan! Open up!"

There I was, knocking down Dan's door at 6 AM. I hadn't gotten a wink of sleep after the drive — but I also didn't feel safe venturing out before dawn.

"Dan!"

After five minutes of constant shouting, thumps resonated from within the house. Dan swung the door open, hair rumpled, looking like he'd just woken up. "Violet! What are you doing here?"

"I saw you at the church. You were there with the rest of them, and..."

"What are you talking about?"

"Around 3 AM, you were standing in the church lawn."

"No, I wasn't." Dan's eyebrows furled in concern. "Are you feeling okay, Violet? You look a bit pale." He reached his hand out and touched my face. "Are you worried about selling your song? I know it's scary, putting creative work in the hands of other people. But I think they'll do a good job with it."

I wasn't listening anymore.

My eyes had fallen on Dan's hands.

They were covered in dirt.

He followed my gaze and looked down at his hands. "What the hell?" he said, staring at his hands. Then he ran over to the sink and began washing them vigorously.

184 | BLAIR DANIELS

I followed him inside. "See? That's what I was saying! You were out there, digging with the rest of them. And it's all because of me. Because you heard my song."

"Violet, you sound crazy. I didn't dig anything, okay? I just got out of bed and answered the door."

"Then where did the dirt come from?"

"I don't know, Violet! Okay? I don't know!"

I fell silent, watching the suds and dirt swirl together in the sink. He turned it off and wiped his hands on a towel.

"You should go. You're going to wake Margot."

I stepped back. In all the years that Dan had been my agent, he never used such a harsh tone with me. Not even when I bungled the song for that perfume commercial.

So I listened to him. I drove home, made coffee, and watched my view count slowly climb to one million.

But at 1 AM, I returned to his house. I parked across the street, turned off my lights, and waited. After more than an hour of freezing to death and eating two expired candy bars, the door creaked open.

Dan exited the house. With slow, ambling footsteps, he descended the porch steps. Then he made a sharp left and started down the street.

I started the car and crawled down the road, headlights off. He walked for a while, then turned left onto Maple Ave.

And that's when I saw it.

A figure, walking several yards ahead of Dan. In the darkness, the silence, going the same direction. Then I noticed the cars — a few of them, driving silently down the street. Like me, they all had their headlights off.

As I got closer to St. Monica's church, more people appeared. More cars appeared. All going the same direction, towards the church. They didn't seem to notice me; apparently, I blended in just fine.

I glanced down at the clock. It was 2:58 AM, and the church was just up ahead.

When I pulled into the church parking lot, I slowly climbed out of the car. I hadn't planned to join them — but now that I was here, I felt the need to. I wanted to know what they were doing.

And if it was, somehow, related to my song.

I walked through the crowd of people that had gathered on the lawn. They might as well have been marble statues. They stared blankly ahead, taking no notice of me. The ones closer to the center of the crowd had already dropped to their knees and started to dig. They'd already made good headway; a large ditch of broken grass, about ten feet in diameter, lay in the center of the lawn.

That's where I found Dan. He was clawing at the dirt frantically, sending clumps of it everywhere.

"Dan! Are you okay?" I asked him. I knew it was a bad idea to engage these people. But I needed to know.

He didn't reply.

"Hey, Dan. I don't know what's wrong with you, but we need to get you home. Okay?"

Still nothing.

I leaned over and grabbed him by the arm. "Come on. Let's go home. You've had enough digging —"

Hot pain shot up my wrist.

Dan gripped my wrist, staring into my eyes with a manic anger. The blank expression was long gone. A few of the other people turned to stare at us.

He dragged me out of the crowd, past the lawn, to the border of the forest. "Dan, what are you doing?" I shouted, tugging against him. "Let go of me. Please."

"We need to find what's *underneath*," he whispered.

"What are you talking about?"

"We need to dig her out."

"Who?"

"The one that sleeps under the earth for eternity. She has waited until now — for this moment, when we free her. She will rain down revenge and pain on our foes, exalt us into kings and queens —"

"Dan! You're hurting me!" His grip on my wrist had grown even tighter.

"With just us, we will never burrow deep enough to reach her. But now..." He trailed off into a wheezing laugh. "In just a few days, the entire *world* will hear your song, and start digging. I made sure of that when I contacted Chained Up."

My heart dropped. The world spun around me.

"You didn't actually write that song, by the way," he said. "It came a little too easy, didn't it? You had to realize that."

"I... I don't know what you mean."

"I knew you had talent. Widespread appeal. You were the perfect vessel, as it were. So after grooming you for years, I put a cassette player under your window. Started playing the song, to put it in your subconscious. Make you think it was your own idea. Worked perfectly."

He finally let go of me. I swayed dangerously close to the ground.

"Great job, Violet. Your best work yet."

He shot me a smile before walking back towards the crowd. I collapsed into the cold, frozen grass, my heart pounding.

What have I done?

188 | BLAIR DANIELS

TINFOIL HAT

Sarah sat across from me, wearing a tinfoil hat.

She'd put effort into it. Tinfoil sculpted neatly around her entire head, with a nice little bulb on the top.

"Can you tell me why you wear that, Sarah?" I asked.

Her eyes darted back and forth, as if the Government – or whatever entity she was afraid of – might hear her. "They'll listen to my thoughts," she finally whispered. "And then..."

"I understand. But 1 can assure you – it's perfectly safe to remove the tinfoil, Sarah."

"Really?"

Poor girl. Her lip was trembling, and her eyes were wide with fear.*What made her so afraid? Of the government, or aliens, or whatever else she thinks is listening in on her thoughts?*We'd already investigated her parents. There was no evidence of any sort of abuse. So why was this little 8-year-old girl so scared?

"I know you think, when you take off that hat, that something will listen in on your thoughts. And then, that'd be a disaster, right? Because maybe the government, or aliens, or whatever else is listening will use that to their advantage. They'll stalk you, or try to control your mind. But that won't happen, Sarah."

"But they'll kill me. When they hear my thoughts, they'll come in the middle of the night and –"

"Ssssh. None of that is going to happen, Sarah. You're okay."

"No, I'm not!" she said, tears brimming in her eyes.

"I promise, you are. There's nothing to be afraid of, okay? Nothing." I leaned forward and gave her a smile. "Can you try to take off the hat?"

"No, I don't want to."

"Please? Try. For me. I promise – nothing bad will happen."

She looked around, her face growing pale. "You*promise?* "

"Promise. I'll even do the pinky thing."

She finally broke into a smile.

Our pinkies locked. Then she slowly reached up for the tinfoil. She shut her eyes tight.

She yanked it off.

I jumped back. My heart pounded in my chest.

"Dr. Taylor? Are you okay?"

A ringing filled my ears. It gave way to whispers – talking all at once, overlapping and hissing. Some fell away, others intensified, until the words became clear:

Take your Swiss Army knife from the cabinet.

Stab her in the eye with it.

Now.

The voice wasn't hers. It was low, deep, rasping. The kind of voice that scrapes at your mind, shredding your sanity.

"Sarah?" I asked. But my voice sounded so small.

And then I felt my body move. I clenched my muscles, tried to stop; but nothing happened. My feet shuffled forward, towards the cabinet.

Towards the knife.

Her eyes widened. She reached down and grabbed the tinfoil, pushed it back over her hair. Immediately – the voices extinguished. A dull ringing throbbed in my ears.

"I'm so sorry," she said, bursting into tears. "I didn't want you to hear it, Dr. Taylor. That's why I didn't want to take it off. That's why –"

"It's okay, Sarah," I said. "You're going to be okay. I promise."

But I wasn't so sure that was a promise I could keep. Because now I knew.

She doesn't wear the hat to keep something out.

She wears it to keep that voice in.

I FOUND MY DOPPELGANGER ON FACEBOOK

Have you ever blocked an ex?

I blocked all of them. Facebook, phone numbers, the whole nine yards. When my husband and I got engaged, it was time to give up my guilty pleasure of stalking exes... no matter how much joy I got from seeing Michael chronically unemployed, or David dating a woman double his age.

I'd successfully avoided stalking them for seven years – until last night. A friend of mine posted a photo of herself at a wedding.

My ex, Joseph's, wedding.

Huh. I felt that familiar twinge in my stomach. Not jealousy, exactly – I was happily married. Just... annoyance? Curiosity? Nostalgia?

Maybe all three.

I unblocked him. Sure enough, his profile photo showed him standing at the altar. Watching his lovely bride walk up the aisle. I couldn't see much from the photo, since her back was turned. But she was curvy, with long, dark hair.

His "type." My type.

Another twinge.

I turned around. Chris was snoring softly, out like a light. *Should I really be doing this? Checking out an ex's wife?* I hadn't seen Joseph in 12 years. I didn't really care about him, or his wife.

Did I?

I couldn't stop myself. I greedily clicked on the album titled *Wedding Photos*. The first image loaded.

I let out a gasp.

The bride... looked *exactly* like me. Dark hair, falling to her waist in soft waves. A pointed chin. Full cheeks. Even that mole on her neck, under her left ear.

It was like looking in a mirror.

I clicked madly through the photos. Through the ceremony, the reception. There she – no, *I* – was, throwing my head back in laughter during our first dance. There I was, closing my eyes, tossing the bouquet behind me. There I was, snuggled up to him, looking out the taxi window.

I would've thought it was some Photoshop trick, but the photos went years back. Us, standing in front of the Eiffel Tower. Baking muffins together. Engagement photos, showing off her ring – with the same freckle I had, near her thumb.

I clicked on her profile. *Anna Brekje.* Sadly, she kept it pretty private. The only thing I could see was her profile picture – a wedding photo I'd already seen.

Before I could stop myself, I clicked on her name and started typing a message.

Hi Anna. My name is Jenna Baker. I saw that you and Joseph got married. Congratulations! How did you two meet?

I didn't point out the fact that we looked like twins. She'd see it herself. No need to be a creep.

The message popped up a second later:

✓ *Seen 12:47 AM*

Then three dancing dots appeared, indicating she was typing a response.

My heart began to pound. I grabbed my glass of wine and took a huge gulp, my fingers slipping against the keyboard.

But a reply never came.

After several minutes, I typed another message, nicer this time:

I'm sorry if this seems like a random message from a stranger. I just wanted to reach out, because I thought it was kind of cool that we looked so much like each other.

✓ *Seen 12:52 AM*

I tapped my fingers across the table, then took another sip of wine. Or, well, tried to. The glass was empty. I got up, poured another from the fridge, and sat back down at the computer.

Still no message.

Around 2 AM, I finally closed the laptop and joined Chris in bed.

She doesn't look exactly like me. That's what I told myself, as I slipped into sleep. *Her eyes are a little too close together. Her smile hitches up on one side. And she's shorter than me, isn't she?* People sometimes look alike. It happens all the time. My cousin looks just like Taylor Swift, when she does her makeup right. Two guys I knew in college – Evan Johnson and Justin Scalzo – looked like brothers.

When there are 7 billion people in the world, some are bound to look alike.

Right?

***

The next day, Anna popped up in my "suggested friends."

I hate it how Facebook does that. You stalk someone, and then suddenly, it suggests them as a potential friend. It's like some sort of stalking hangover.

I nearly scrolled past the friend suggestion, when I saw the text under her name:

12 mutual friends

She'd had no mutual friends with me last night.

What the hell? I read the names. *Molly Ackerfield, Jesslyn Johns, Mike Zhu...* They weren't people I'd talked to recently, but they weren't just random acquaintances, either. Molly had been my freshman roommate in college, Jesslyn worked a few cubicles down at my last job, and Mike was an old crush of mine from high school.

I saw that Mike was online and shot him a message.

me: Hey Mike. Did you accept a friend request by someone named 'Anna Brekje'?

Mike: Oh hey! You got your account back!

Did you find out who hacked it?

me: No one hacked my account. What are you talking about?

Mike: You messaged me from that Anna account saying it was your new one. That your old one had gotten hacked. And you were using a new name because you were sick of your boss checking up on your FB.

me: That's not me.

Mike: But the picture is of you.

I clicked over to her profile. Her picture was no longer a photo from the wedding – it was just a plain old selfie. No makeup, morning light, with the caption "New day. New me." I squinted at the background; it looked familiar, somehow. Blue sky, a patch of grass, and the corner of a stone building. But I couldn't quite place it.

I shook off the feeling and continued typing to Mike.

me: That's not me, Mike.

Mike: Oh, it's a bot?

I didn't know how to explain everything. So I told him yes, and to unfriend her immediately. Then I messaged the other eleven people and told them the same thing. I poured myself a cup of coffee – it was too early for wine – and sat back down at the computer, staring at her face.

"What are you up to?"

I jumped at Chris's voice. He stood behind me, smiling, still in his pajamas.

"Just browsing Facebook," I said, shutting the computer. "But I should get to work. I'm going to be late."

I wanted to tell him about it. But then I'd have to admit to stalking Joseph, and spending hours tracking down his wife...

After a quiet breakfast, I made my way over. The rain was driving down in sheets, drowning out the surrounding noise. I found the sound calming – water hitting the glass, over and over, washing away my fear.

I pulled into the parking lot.

No.

Next to the door stood a figure. Her face was hidden under a black umbrella – but familiar waves of dark hair fell down her waist.

I swung the car door open and swiftly walked towards her.

"Anna?" I called.

She didn't look at me. Instead, she turned around and walked down the sidewalk. Then she disappeared into the far end of the parking lot.

"Hey, you okay?"

My coworker, Lena, leaned against the stone building. In one hand, she held a Starbucks cup; in the other, her phone. I hadn't even noticed her.

"Did you see that woman?"

"What woman?"

I shook my head. "Nevermind."

Get a hold of yourself.

That wasn't even her.

You're driving yourself crazy.

I took a deep breath and followed Lena into the building. We entered the elevator and I closed my eyes, determined to put this behind me and get some work done.

***

My phone was gone.

In my rush to pursue what I thought was Anna, I'd left my phone in the car. And my wallet. And forgotten to lock it up.

Now they were both gone.

Nothing else was missing. Not even the $30 cash in my glove compartment.

I swung into the driver's seat. My shirt was soaked with rain. I gripped the steering wheel and began to cry.

It was too much stress. This weird woman who looked just like me, now my stuff getting stolen... it was one of the worst weeks I'd had in a long time. I needed to tell Chris everything. He'd know what to do. He was always my rock, my calming force. Whenever I spiraled into anxiety, he was always there to pull me back.

I turned up the radio and drove home.

But when I pulled into our driveway, I found a car already there. A blue Honda Civic – just like mine.

I slowly got out of the car. Walked up to our door, my heart hammering in my chest.

I heard voices inside.

"That was fantastic! I didn't know you knew how to make chicken cacciatore."

A giggle.

My giggle.

I pulled out my keys. But my house key was missing from the keyring. I backed away from the door, feeling dizzy, and walked around the side of the house.

I peered through the window.

Through a gap in the curtains, I could see them. Chris clearing the plates. His eyes twinkling as he stared at *her*. She sat at the table, her back turned to me. I could just make out her hair, the vague curve of her face.

I slammed my hand into the glass. "Chris!" I shouted. "It's me!"

But he was already halfway to the kitchen with a pile of dirty plates.

Only *she* heard me.

She whipped around. Dark eyes locking on mine.

My heart stopped. She looked exactly like me – yet so, so different. She sat up straighter than I did, and her movements were too smooth, too graceful. The expression she wore – a small, mischievous smile that didn't reach her eyes – was one I'd never wear.

How could Chris not see the difference?

Keeping her eyes on mine, she reached down and pulled something out of her purse. The black metal glinted in the light, and I panicked.

A revolver.

She's going to shoot me.

But then she turned – and pointed the revolver directly at Chris. He was hunched over the sink, his back to us, utterly oblivious.

"No. Please, no," I whispered, my voice shaking with tears.

She lowered the gun.

Then go, she mouthed.

I backed away from the house. Footsteps thumped, and I heard his voice again. I was too far away to make out the words, but I could hear his light, lilting tone. My heart ached. More footsteps sounded, and then I saw a light turn on upstairs.

Our bedroom.

My insides twisted. Nausea bubbled up in my throat.

But I dutifully opened my car door, got inside, and drove away.

Now, I'm at a hotel. I've been here for the past few hours, pacing and panicking, not sure what to do. I can't go back to the house. She'll shoot him. I can call the police, but she has my wallet. My phone. She can prove that she is Jenna Baker, through and through.

And then she might kill Chris anyway.

Because I know she wasn't just making empty threats.

According to Facebook, Joseph passed away last night. His profile is overrun with condolences and memories. Friends and family alike, celebrating his life, mourning the loss of a beautiful soul.

The top post is from Anna herself.

I'm so sorry I couldn't be there for you, Joseph. I wish I could have reassured you. Shown you how much you are loved. Been by your side, through and through.

I wish you didn't take your own life.

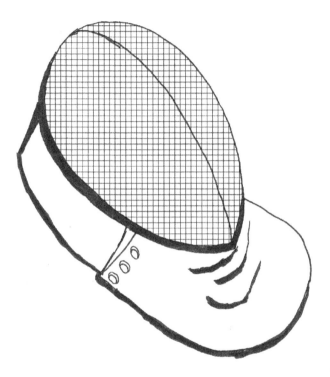

THE FENCING MASK

I pulled up my sword. It shimmered in the lights, silver and sleek.

"En garde!"

Adam had bested me in two out of our three matches. I was eager to get one more win in before we closed up for the night. I lunged forward with my épée, hitting Adam squarely in the chest.

"Nice one," Adam said, as we ended the round. "That even hurt a bit."

I grabbed my water bottle. "I've been practicing."

"Oh yeah? With whom?"

"Strangers. I just walk up behind them and start stabbing them." I thrust my sword into the open air. "I'm very good at stabbing."

He stared at me, mortified.

Then we broke into laughter. "How about another round?" he asked, pulling the mask back over his face. "Tiebreaker. Come on."

"Alright, alright." I put down my water and pulled the mask back down.

That's when I saw it.

A flash of movement. Dark and blurry, just out the corner of my eye. The dark mesh of the mask obscured it, so I couldn't tell what it was—or if I'd even seen it at all.

"Geoff? Are you okay?"

I yanked the mask off, glanced around. The club was empty. The linoleum floors glistened under the fluorescent lights, and the room was quiet. "Yeah... I'm fine."

He narrowed his eyes at me, skeptically. Before he could say anything, I pulled the mask back down and shouted: "en garde!"

The épées clashed together with a metallic *ting.* We danced across the linoleum as we advanced and retreated, lunged and blocked. I thrust the sword at Adam—

And stopped.

There it was, again. A flutter of movement. I signaled at Adam to stop, then took off my mask. "Is someone else here?"

"Nope. The club is technically closed, remember? Eugene just gives me a spare key."

My gaze fell on the supply room. The door hung open. *Had it been open before?* "I'm just going to check the supply room. Okay?"

"You think someone's hiding out in there?" Adam smiled at me and shook his head. "You watch too many horror movies, my man."

I rolled my eyes at him and made my way across the floor. Heart pounding, I poked my head inside.

It appeared empty. Well, empty of *people*, at least. Inside, the shelves overflowed with fencing equipment. Masks, plasterons, jackets, swords. A few plastic containers were lined up on the floor, filled to the brim with equipment. At the far wall, Eugene had three mannequins, to show off his best equipment: pristine jackets, pants, masks. One, I noticed, was even complete with a pair of shoes.

"Okay. You're right. I'm going crazy," I said, with an uneasy laugh, as I rejoined Adam. "There's nothing there."

"No worries." He reached up to his mask and grinned. "Ready to be *utterly demolished?!*"

"Actually, I'm going to get some water first." My mouth was dry, and my heart was still racing.

"Sure thing."

I grabbed my empty bottle and walked over to the bathroom to refill it.

Drip, drip, drip. Drops of water fell from the sink on the right, hitting the ceramic. I turned it on and filled the water bottle. As I sipped from it, I stared at my reflection. *Adam's right. I'm getting too paranoid.* It was only last week that I'd been convinced there was someone screaming in the woods behind my house.

Then my neighbor told me it was just the foxes, and I felt like an idiot.

Maybe I should cut back on the horror movies. I'm thinking every little noise, every little motion is a serial killer waiting to jump out at me.

I capped the water bottle and headed back into the main room.

Adam was already waiting for me, mask on. I put down my bottle, pulled the mask back over my face, and said: "En guarde!"

The club once again filled with the clangs of metal. In seconds, I realized my hope of winning the tiebreaker was horribly misguided. He *was* "utterly demolishing" me, and it was embarrassing.

I brought my sword up to block him. But then he stepped to the side, slashed through the air, and hit me squarely in the shoulder.

Pain shot through me. I reeled back.

It *hurt*—more than the usual bit of pressure and pain that accompanies a hit. "Hey, can we stop for a minute?" I said through the mask, holding up a hand. He didn't reply.

I glanced down at his sword.

Holy shit.

It wasn't Adam's usual épée. The safety knob was gone... and the end was razor sharp. *Holy shit.* I backed up. "Adam! Stop! Your épée!"

He must've not heard me.

Because he advanced.

Swiftly, nimbly, thrusting the sword at me with insane speed. He aimed for my chest—I blocked it at the last second—then I backed up.

"What the hell are you doing?!" I shouted, stepping further back. "I said stop! There's something wrong with your épée—"

My back hit the wall.

I was cornered.

He stabbed at my chest. I tried to block it—but I wasn't quite successful. The sword grazed my unprotected arm, slicing right through the skin with searing pain. Red blood filled the cut, and I winced.

But he didn't stop. He raised the sword, aiming for me again, and I realized—

That's not Adam.

The blank, expressionless mask stared down at me.

I ducked and rolled to the side. The épée hit the wall with a sharp scraping sound. I ran across the floor, dread growing in my chest, pressing on my lungs. *Where the hell is Adam?*

I heard a low groan from my left.

The supply room.

I ducked inside and closed the door. There, on the floor, lay Adam. Blood staining his white uniform. I quickly dragged one of the heavy equipment containers in front of the door.

"Adam! Adam, what—"

"He came up behind me," he groaned. "I'm okay—I think. He only got my leg… he heard you, and pushed me in the closet."

"We need to get out of here." I glanced around the room. The two mannequins at the back, the heaps of equipment, the swords... then my eyes fell on the right wall. The window.

Thump!

A loud sound came through the door. It shook. The equipment container shifted a half-inch across the floor.

"Go!" I wrenched the window open and punched out the screen. Then I helped Adam through. *Thump!* The door shook again, and I pushed myself out—

Snap!

The door burst open.

The fencer stepped in. Watching me from behind that dark mask. He bounded forward, sword out. Seconds before he got to me, I pulled through the window. I grabbed Adam by the shoulders, helped him up, and stumbled across the parking lot.

He didn't follow.

We dove inside the car. I started the car and backed up. As we peeled out of the parking space, I stared at the club.

The figure stood in the window, watching us.

THE PUMPKIN

There's a tapping sound coming from our pumpkin.

I only hear it when the kitchen is totally silent. When the dishwasher isn't running, the fan is off, and my son isn't screaming.

Tap-tap-tap.

We got the pumpkin yesterday, from one of those "Pick Your Own" patches. James chose it. We first heard it right after we'd pulled into our driveway and turned the engine off.

Tap-tap-tap.

"Is that the car?" I asked my husband.

He shrugged.

"It's the pumpkin!"

We turned around to see James with his ear pressed against the pumpkin, a huge grin on his face. "It's a magic one!"

Tyler and I gave each other a look. *Probably bugs,* he mouthed at me. Then, in a sickly-sweet voice, called back to James: "That's great! A magic pumpkin! Wow!"

After James went to sleep, we devised a plan to get rid of the pumpkin. "The thing's probably all rotten on the inside, with maggots and stuff. I'll get rid of it."

"James will freak when he notices it's missing."

"You underestimate me, dear Maggie," he said, a sly smile creeping onto his face. He opened the pantry and pulled out a nearly identical pumpkin. "I got this earlier today. He'll probably cry over the fact that it isn't making noise anymore, but it's better than the alternative."

Tap-tap-tap—the soft, hollow sound echoed through the kitchen.

I walked over to the pumpkin and took a closer look. That's when I noticed a thin crack in one of the grooves. "It's cracked," I said.

"Probably because it's rotting."

"Great."

The crack ran down the entire length of the pumpkin, across the bottom, and up the other side. As if the pumpkin had been split open completely at one point. But when I tugged gently at the halves, it didn't open.

"Okay. Let's get rid of this thing." Tyler took the pumpkin and disappeared outside.

But, the next morning, I woke up to two pumpkins sitting on the floor. James sat in front of them, grinning, holding his ear up to each. "This one is magic," he said. "That one isn't."

"Tyler!" I shouted.

He poked his head out of the family room. "Yeah?"

I stormed in and lowered my voice. "I thought you got rid of the P-U-M-P-K-I-N."

"I did. I thought *you* brought it back."

"Me? I've been sleeping this whole time!"

He stared at me, brown eyes suddenly fearful. "Well, I didn't bring it back."

"Do you think James found it?"

"Maybe. I did leave it only a few feet from the door."

"You didn't throw it in the woods?"

"It's heavy!" he protested.

I turned back to James. He was crouched over the pumpkins, tapping his finger against the orange flesh. Trying to imitate the sound he heard inside.

I charged over and grabbed the pumpkin.

"Hey!"

"I'm sorry, James, but this pumpkin is all rotten and yucky on the inside. We have to throw it away, okay?"

"I want the magic pumpkin!" he screamed, starting to cry.

"No, James—"

"Give it back!" he shrieked, tugging at my pants.

I glanced at Tyler. He shrugged.

"Okay. Fine." I plopped the pumpkin down and charged out of the room. "We'll get rid of it tonight," I whispered.

After James went to sleep, we had the same exact discussion. "I got this third pumpkin at the store," I said, rolling it out onto the countertop. "Let's get rid of the *magic* one, now."

"Which one is it, again?"

"...I forget."

We fell silent and listened.

Tap-tap-tap. The soft sound came through the one on the left. I leaned in and listened. *Tap-tap-tap.* A scraping sound, too. As if something were getting caught on the spongey insides.

"It's this one."

I picked it up. *Tap-tap-tap.* I could feel the vibrations from the tapping against my hand, and I shuddered.

We walked out into the backyard, opened the gate, and continued towards the edge of the woods. I raised my arms to chuck it as hard as I could—but Tyler stopped me. "Wait."

"What?"

"Do you want to see what's inside?"

I frowned at him. "Not really."

"Oh, come on. Aren't you morbidly curious? Like is it maggots, or an earwig, or—"

"Ew! Geez, Tyler!"

"Come on. Let's crack it open and find out."

I scowled at him in the moonlight. He grinned, walked back up to our garage, and came back with an axe.

"Okay. You ready?" he asked, lifting the axe up.

"No."

He paused—then swung it down as hard as he could. *Crack*—the flesh started to split. The tapping sound grew louder. Frenzied. *Tap-tap-tap-tap-tap.*

He swung it down again.

CRACK!

The pumpkin split open.

My heart stopped. Every muscle in my body froze.

There, lying in the moonlight—among the orange shards of pumpkin—was a severed human hand.

I CHOSE MY CHILD

We chose the gender of our third child.

We already had two boys, and the last thing I wanted was *another* shouting, biting, Lightning-McQueen-obsessed toddler. I could already imagine curling up with her on the couch with a good book, while the boys flung dirt at each other.

Our sweet little girl.

Then, we found a company called "BabyLabs." They claimed gender selection with 95% accuracy—much higher than the other companies we'd looked at. And cheaper.

"Please fill this form out," the secretary said when we arrived, handing us a clipboard. I grabbed a pen and began to fill out our name and address. Then I turned the page.

Please answer the following questions about your ideal child.

Gender: M F

I circled F, then moved onto the next item.

Eye Color: blue green hazel brown other:____

"What? You can choose eye color?" I muttered to Ethan.

He leaned over and glanced at the page. "I guess so. The marvels of modern science, huh?"

"Yeah," I said, half-heartedly. Something about choosing the eye color didn't sit right with me. But I moved on to the next question, pen tapping against the page.

And my heart began to pound.

Widow's Peak: yes no
Earlobes: attached free
Height: short average tall

"Is that even possible? Genetically determine... *all* of those things?"

"I guess so. They know what genes control those traits, right? Like on 23andme and all those ancestry sites. They must just use that information to create an embryo with those traits."

"Or make a thousand embryos, and destroy the nine-hundred ninety-nine that don't have them."

"I... guess."

Dread settled in my stomach. But I continued to read.

Creativity: ___ (select number from 0 to 100)

Intelligence Quotient (IQ):   <85   85-100   100-115 115-130 >130 or, please specify:_____

Myers-Briggs Personality (circle one for each category): E I, S N, T F, J P

What? This was more than just gender selection. This was... *ordering* a child. And it was absolutely insane. I threw the clipboard on the table and stood up. "This is crazy. Let's get out of here and—"

I stopped.

The secretary was staring at me. A warning glare— as if she were daring me to finish that sentence. Ethan grabbed my arm and gently pulled me back down.

"Samantha, we don't have to do any of those other things. We'll just select the gender and that's it."

"Then we should do it somewhere else."

"Come on. This place has 95% accuracy. And it's cheap." Ethan took my hands in his. "Do you really want to give up on our dream of having a little girl?"

"Maybe I do. Maybe this whole thing is insane."

But he eventually persuaded me. Not that day. Not even that week. But within the month, we were back at BabyLab, telling the secretary we wanted a little girl.

No other selections.

Just gender.

***

A year later, our baby Charlotte was born.

From day one she was a wonderful baby. She slept well, ate well, and didn't even cry that often. I could tell she was going to be a piece of cake to raise compared to the boys.

A year went by. Then two, then three, then four. She was growing up to be a wonderful little girl. I spent so many evenings reading to her on the porch, as the boys smeared God-knows-what on each other's faces. She was the only one in the family to inherit my mom's blue eyes, and it seemed she inherited her grace, poise, and manners as well.

Then, when she was four-and-a-half, everything began to fall apart.

I remember the day clearly. It's seared into my brain, as if pressed in with a hot iron. After I fed the cat, I walked over to the playroom to check on them. The boys were hitting each other with stuffed dinosaurs, and Charlotte was in the corner, playing with the Barbies in her dollhouse.

"Are you having fun with your dolls, Charlotte?"

"Yes, Mommy."

"Can I play?"

"Sure!"

I crouched to her level—and froze.

One Barbie's head was thrust into the fireplace. Another was laying upside-down on the stairs. The Ken doll was dangling off the balcony. And the last one... its body was sitting in the armchair, and its head was on the dinner table.

"Charlotte? What is this?" I said, trying to fake a smile. *It can't be what it looks like.*

"They're dying."

"Charlotte! That... you can't..." I faltered. "Ethan!"

He came running in. His eyes widened as soon as he saw the dollhouse scene. And then, *of course,* the boys came over in a whir of blond hair and stuffed dinosaurs. "Woah! That one doesn't have a head!" Davie said. "What's happening to them?!" Johnny asked.

Oh my gosh. This is a disaster.

Ethan and I gave an impromptu talk about why it *wasn't* a good idea to play out the dolls' violent deaths. At the end of it, Charlotte promised she wouldn't, and the boys were mischievously giggling.

I hoped that would be the end of it.

Unfortunately, it was just the beginning.

A few days later, I found our cat dead. She was lying in the center of the backyard, gashes all over her body. The way they were placed suggested precision. Not the random claw marks of a frenzied animal.

I showed Ethan after the kids were asleep. "I don't think an animal did this," I said, wincing as I dropped the stiff body in a shallow grave.

He raised an eyebrow at me in the darkness. "What are you implying? That the cat was *murdered?*"

"No. Just..." I trailed off. What *was* I implying? Even I didn't know.

That night I barely slept a wink. Pieces were coming together in my mind, threatening to burst through the wall of my subconscious. I felt like I already knew, but I couldn't quite fit the pieces together, couldn't quite grasp what exactly it was.

The next day, I decided to busy myself with cleaning. While the boys were at school and Charlotte was coloring in the family room, I got to work. I deposited the cars in several boxes, organized by brand (Hot Wheels in one, *Cars* cars in another.) Then I got to work on the doll house. Grabbing a damp rag, I began to wipe the plastic down.

Something silver glinted back at me, nestled behind the plastic couches in the miniature family room. *What is that?* I reached my hand inside and slowly pulled it out.

My heart dropped. Every muscle in my body froze.

It was one of our steak knives.

"Charlotte!" I yelled. I heard her footsteps patter slowly on the floor before she poked her head in.

"Yes, Mommy?"

"What is this doing in your dollhouse?"

"I wanted the dolls to eat," she said, her blue eyes sparkling with innocence. "They couldn't cut their food."

I narrowed my eyes at her, and walked back into the kitchen. "You're not supposed to play with knives. You *know* that!" I said, dropping the knife in the drawer with the other silverware. "Don't do it again, okay?"

"Okay, Mommy." She looked at me with a pout. "Are you mad at me?"

"No. Just... disappointed," I said. She smiled and ran off to finish coloring.

I told Ethan as soon as he got home. "She had a *knife,*" I whispered, pulling him aside.

He shrugged. "So?"

"What do you mean, *so?* I think—the cat—"

"Are you implying she killed the cat?!"

"Maybe."

"You think our *four year old daughter* murdered our cat?!" He shook his head. "Samantha, that's ridiculous."

"Something isn't right with her. The way she set up those dolls—the way she looks at me—there's something wrong, and I—"

"You what?"

"I think this is our punishment. For choosing the gender of our child. I *told* you, I wanted to leave. I'd changed my mind. But you persuaded me to do it anyway. I know we only chose the gender, but still, the entire thing—"

"Samantha." Ethan no longer looked angry. In fact, he looked guilty, with the way he averted my eyes. "We didn't... *just...* choose the gender."

"What are you talking about?"

"I, uh... I added some choices. It was the same price, so—"

My eyes locked on his. "*What?!*"

"I chose her eye color. Blue. And her IQ. 155. And her personality—very creative, innovative. Those were the only things, I swea—"

"I can't believe you!" I screamed. I ran up the stairs, leaving him alone with the kids.

I didn't go out. I couldn't face him. I heard him singing songs and reading books as he put the kids to bed. Soon after that, I finally fell asleep, too tired to be angry anymore.

I woke up with a jolt at 2:31 AM.

As I faded into consciousness, I became aware of a sound. A voice, coming from downstairs.

I opened the door and crept down the stairs. The glow of a lamp fell over the carpet, spilling out from the open playroom door. I walked over and pushed the door open.

Charlotte was sitting on the floor beside her dollhouse.

In front of her, there were four dolls lined up on the carpet. A Barbie doll with black hair like mine, a Ken, and two blonde Barbies she'd chopped the hair of.

Humming to herself, she raised the same kitchen knife I'd taken back from her earlier. *Snap!* She brought it down on the neck of the first doll. The head popped off, rolled across the floor. "Mommy," she whispered under her breath.

Then she resumed humming—and raised the knife over the next doll.

THE BIRDS

My new house is surrounded by birds.

They all perch on the oak tree right outside my bedroom window. About a dozen of them, watching me with those mean little black eyes.

"Hey birdies!" I've said to them, many times, waving my arms.

But they never move. They just sit and watch me.

I eventually decided to accept them. I mean, I'm a single girl living alone; I could use some company. As a peace offering, I hauled my butt to the store and bought them a bird feeder.

They never ate from it.

After that, I forgot about them for a while. Sometimes I'd hear their song out my window—the very same tune, at eight AM sharp. *Chip chip chipchip cheeeeeeeeep.* But for the most part, they were just... *there.*

It all went to shit when I got a cat.

Cat and birds don't mix. You probably know this, but me—as a first-time cat owner—didn't really think it through. As soon as I brought her home, she permanently stationed herself in my bedroom window.

I expected them to fly away. But the birds just stared back at her.

The first night, Butters stayed up far past bedtime, stationed at the window. "Come on. Let's go to sleep," I groaned, joining her at the window. "What are you even looking at? All the birds have gone to sleep."

I froze.

The birds were there. Perched in the branches. Black eyes glittering in the darkness.

Why are they still up?

I pulled the curtains closed and brought Butters to her bed. "No more birdies. Sleep, now."

She mewled in protest.

The next day, I let her out in the yard. I meant to watch her explore her new surroundings, but then I got a call from my mom.

"How's the cat?"

"She's great," I said, walking back into the house. "She loves watching the birds out my window." I glanced out the door to see Butters sitting under the tree, staring up at the birds as we spoke.

"Oh, how sweet."

We talked for several minutes. When I hung up and walked to the back door, Butters was no longer at the tree.

"Butters! Where are you?"

She came bounding out of the bushes on my right.

With one of the birds in her teeth.

"Butters! No!" I shouted. The cat proudly dumped the carcass at my feet. A sad clump of ruffled gray feathers.

Looking awfully proud of herself, she strutted back inside.

"Eugh," I muttered. I couldn't exactly leave the thing on my patio, though. I had to get rid of it. I followed her in and put on some gloves. Then, with a sigh, I bent over to pick up the bird.

It was heavier than I expected it to be. *Much* heavier. I brought it up to my face to get a closer look.

That's when I noticed the wire.

A twisted red wire, jutting out from its broken neck. *What the hell?* I pulled back the feathers to get a closer look.

I froze.

Its body was filled with metal. Wires. Green circuitry.

And its eyes... were two tiny cameras.

THE HAUNTING OF ROOM 812

by *Blair Daniels & Craig Groshek*

It was the most haunted room in all of South Dakota. Haunted by the lady in white – a bride who was left at the altar, and jumped from the window to her death.

Or, if you asked some... a woman who was brutally murdered by her husband-to-be.

"Are you picking up anything?" Darren asked, staring at his K2 meter.

"Nope," I replied. "No activity so far."

"How about you?"

Darren turned to Annabelle, the red-headed woman holding the camcorder. "No," she said, looking at the screen. "Nothing."

"Let's go in, then, and see if we get anything."

I pulled out my keycard and shoved it into the door. The lock clicked, and I pushed the door open.

The room was dark. And cold. My hand skimmed the wall, searching for a light switch. Even as a "ghost hunter," I didn't like walking into totally dark, strange rooms.

The lights flicked on and we found ourselves in what appeared to be a normal room. Perfectly-made bed, small windows, cream-colored walls.

We all stared at our meters, and cameras, for a good hour. Unfortunately, not so much as a glowing speck of dust made its appearance. Darren was the first to give up – he groaned in disappointment and flopped onto the bed. "Man, we're not getting any breaks here, are we?"

"Nope, and I was *sure* we'd catch something," I grumbled. "This stinks."

My thoughts weren't on spooky ghosts, but our dwindling YouTube ad revenue. Every ghost-hunting video we posted garnered fewer views. We *needed* this. One blurry silhouette, one bout of flickering lights, one chair moving on its own accord. *Something.*

"Maybe it's time we hire a video editor," Darren said, staring blankly at the meter. "I mean, all the other channels do it. Add a little blur, some glowing orbs—"

"No! Our whole *thing* is that our videos are real. We don't Photoshop. We don't edit. We post *real* stuff only." I crossed my arms and glared at him. "You want to sell out? Resort to forgeries?"

"I want to be able to pay my rent," he said into the pillow. "And eat something other than ramen."

"Guys. Ssshhh."

Annabelle brought a finger to her lips. The tinny ding of the elevator pierced the silence, followed by heavy footfalls outside.

"Someone's coming off the elevator," Darren said. "What's the big deal?"

"It's 1 AM," Annabelle whispered. "Who'd be up this late on a Tuesday night?"

The three of us swarmed the peephole. From what I could see, the elevator doors were open. And I heard faint footsteps.

But no one was there.

"Probably just some guy going down to get a snack," Darren said.

"Looks like this place really is just a tourist trap," I said, spinning the hotel pen between my fingers. "Just like most 'haunted places' are."

"The night's not over yet, boys," Annabelle said. But her tone wasn't very convincing.

We returned to our stations around the room. Annabelle set her camera on a tripod and remained filming, but pulled out a tabloid magazine and turned her attention to that instead. Darren played games on his phone. I collapsed on the bed and stared at the ceiling.

The hours ticked by. Around 3 AM, Annabelle caught a glowing orb on film. But, upon closer inspection, we realized it was just a mosquito flying near the lens. "We've gotten better footage in the Wal-Mart parking lot," Darren complained. "This blows."

It was around 4 AM that things started to get interesting.

At exactly 4:11, the familiar '*ding*' of the elevator sounded again, followed by the same heavy footsteps. Annabelle leapt up and pressed her eye against the peephole.

"Guys! Guys, come here!"

We crowded around. The elevator and the hallway were both empty. The footsteps, however, sounded like they were inches from our door.

She flung the door open. We walked out, cameras out and recording. As soon as we did, the footsteps ceased. But, strangely, the elevator doors remained open.

Annabelle ran inside and motioned for us to follow. "Keep recording!" she said, breathlessly. "I feel like there's something... *here.*"

My gaze fell on the elevator buttons.

The buttons for the third, fifth, and seventh floors suddenly lit up at once. Without being pressed.

"Did you see that?!" I cried.

Darren and Annabelle nodded.

"A haunted elevator, huh. That wasn't in our research."

"Of course not," Annabelle said, as the elevator slid to a halt at the seventh floor. The doors opened with a whoosh, and the empty hallway presented itself. "The Alex Johnson Hotel wants tourists to get creeped out and buy their spooky little ghost package. They don't want tourists to hurt themselves communing with an actual spirit." Her eyes met mine. "Or worse."

"Why's it only stopping at odd-numbered floors? The third floor is where Alex Johnson lived... but why the fifth? Why the seventh?"

Annabelle shook her head. "I have no idea."

"Or, this whole elevator business is the result of a technical malfunction, and the floors are chosen at random."

"Shut up, Darren!" Annabelle said, rolling her eyes. "The elevator is haunted. I can *feel* it."

We came to a stop at the fifth floor. The doors parted, revealing an empty hallway that looked exactly like the hallway on the seventh and eighth floors. Then they quietly slid shut, and the elevator descended. This time, it seemed to go twice as fast as before. I gripped the bar, steadying myself.

Another high-pitched 'ding' signaled our arrival, and the doors slid open.

"What the *hell*?"

The third floor was *dark*.

Not completely, I'll admit. There was a dim light coming from *somewhere*—but it was much darker than any other floor we'd stopped on. I could barely make out the beige carpeting, the cream walls, and the doors extending into the distance.

"Holy crap!" Darren said in disbelief. "Are you getting this?"

I peered at my camera's viewfinder. In it, the floor was fully-lit, and identical to every other floor we'd stopped on. "No, that's impossible," I said, my mouth growing dry. "I, uh... there's something wrong. It looks normal on the screen..."

I looked back up, and nearly had a heart attack.

A figure stood, barely visible, at the end of the hallway, its head canted to the side, as if out of curiosity. It was unsettling, how perfectly it blended into the shadows.

"There's... there's someone out there!" I whispered hoarsely. Instinctively, my hand reached for the 'Close Doors' button on the elevator.

The doors didn't close. The elevator didn't respond at all.

The specter continued to stare at us, its head cocked at an unnatural angle. It was too dark to make out anything else about them. Their hair, their clothes, their gender... it was impossible to tell.

I only knew one thing.

They were getting closer.

I reached for the elevator button. My fingers touched the plastic.

And then I flew forward.

I crashed hard into the carpet, the air rushing from my lungs. I sucked in a choking breath, and tried to regain my composure.

The elevator doors were closing. And in the quickly-narrowing gap, I saw Annabelle and Darren's faces, staring back at me with an odd combination of horror and satisfaction.

"Wait!" I screamed, frantically clambering to my feet.

I was too late. My hands fell on closed doors. I pounded my fists against them – they didn't budge.

I was trapped.

I whipped around, my heart pounding. The wraith was gone.

"Okay..." I reasoned aloud, "Just call back the elevator, and everything will be fine." I turned back to the elevator.

The call button was gone.

Where it had once been, a blank wall surrounded the doors.

"What the *hell is going on?!*" I shouted.

My only option was to make my way back to our room the old-fashioned way. The stairs.

With a nervous gulp, I traversed the dimly-lit hallway, half-expecting the closed doors flanking me on either side to burst open at any moment. An odd static buzzing came from behind some of them, like the sound of thousands of flies struggling against their restraints.

As I passed one of the doors, I heard the muffled voice of a man. Maybe he knew where I could find a working elevator. I wasn't looking forward to walking up five flights of stairs.

"I've been tryin'!" I overheard them say. "I've been tryin' to leave for three days, and I –"

I raised my fist and knocked. As soon as I did, the voice abruptly cut off. I waited, staring at the door.

That's when I noticed the numbers hanging on his door – 308 – were upside-down.

The door cracked open, revealing the sliver of a wild eye glaring back at me. It was that of an old man, from what I could tell. The deep wrinkles of his face were bathed in shadow, making it look as if he'd been carved from wood.

"You're not one of *them,*" he growled, as if it were some sort of shocking revelation.

"Uh... no? Listen, I came down the elevator but there doesn't seem to be a call button down here. Do you know if there's another elevator?" I glanced around, at the dark hallway. "And why are the lights so dim on this floor?"

He stared at me for a moment.

"Get out!" he rasped. "Get out before it's too late!"

"What–"

"Find a door! A window! *Anything!* And get out!"

The door slammed in my face.

Confused, and slightly disturbed, I continued down the hallway. The lights dimmed nearly to the point of extinguishing, flickering softly in their glass bulbs. Over and over I lost my bearings, unable to determine which direction I was going. For what felt like an eternity, I felt my way along the walls, desperately trying to find my way, until finally I arrived at the stairs. Then I began the long, hard climb to the eighth floor.

With every step, the man's words echoed in my mind. *Get out. Get out.* What did he mean by that?

And the figure in the hallway... I'd been ghost hunting for five years, and I'd never seen something like that. Standard fare included glowing orbs, odd tapping sounds, shadowy figures in the corner of my eye. Things that could, technically, be explained away by logic.

This couldn't.

By the time I got to the top, I was panting, and sweat clung to my shirt. I pulled the door open with a groan, and walked down the hallway.

The hallway was dark. Just like the third floor.

It must be some sort of hotel-wide power problem, I told myself. That actually made me feel *better.* Maybe everything that happened – the elevator buttons, the dim lights – was due to an electrical issue. It was an old hotel, after all.

Maybe, in all the confusion, I'd imagined the shadows. And the old man was just some lunatic.

I walked down the hallway, my shoes thumping conspicuously against the carpet. The silence was ominous, though not unexpected. After all, I reasoned, everyone was sleeping at this hour.

I arrived at room 812 and inserted my key card into the door. The lock clicked, and I pushed the door open.

The room was pitch-black, even though I was sure we'd kept every light on when we left.

"Annabelle?" I called. "Darren? You here? We need to talk!"

Silence.

I walked down the short hallway, into the main room—and froze in my tracks.

Frigid air rushed in through the open window. On the windowsill, surrounded by billowing curtains, there stood a feminine figure, facing away from me, wearing a white wedding dress.

"Hey!" I called out to her. "What are you doing in our roo–"

The words were barely out of my mouth when she pitched forward. I heard the soft rustle of fabric and the whistling wind as she plummeted towards the ground.

Then, with the sickening crack of flesh against pavement, everything went still.

Nausea washed over me. I fought the urge to vomit.

I pulled out my phone and dialed Annabelle, my fingers nervously slipping over the screen, and was met with a busy signal. Same for Darren, and for the police. Each and every time, I failed to get through. Then my eyes fell on the hotel phone.

I ran over to it and dialed 'zero' for the front desk. It rang. A moment later, a man's voice answered.

"Hello?"

It all came rushing out. "Oh, thank God! Listen, I need your help! I just saw this woman–she jumped–and I can't find my friends, and–"

"Come to the front desk," he responded in a slow drawl.

Then the line went dead.

I stared into the abyss of the desolate room. Then I got up, averted my gaze from the window, and walked back down all eight flights of stairs.

When I finally wandered into the lobby, I found it deserted. The only faces I encountered were decorative and inanimate. The Alex Johnson Hotel had no less than six faces, wearing feathered headdresses, carved into the beams of the hotel. When I looked up, I could swear I saw a flash of darkness in the balcony overhead. In an instant, however, it was gone.

I ran toward the front desk. "Is anyone here?!" I shouted.

"Hello!" a voice called out of the darkness.

A man bustled out of the back. Portly, middle-aged, with a carefully curled mustache and a pair of round glasses. "What may I help you with?" he asked, lips curling into a smile.

"I just called from upstairs. Someone just jumped from the eighth floor win—"

"Not to worry," he said, cutting me off. His eyes locked on mine. "She does that every night."

"I'm sorry, but... what?" I responded incredulously.

"My dear boy, if you haven't noticed... you're not in South Dakota anymore."

I looked around. "That's ridiculous! Of course I am. This is the Alex Johnson Hotel. What are you talking about?"

"It certainly *looks* like the Alex Johnson Hotel, doesn't it?" he said, casting an adoring glance at the ceiling. "Ah, yes. The attention to detail is remarkable. We have Agneta to thank for that. Lovely woman. Have you met her yet?"

"Listen. You tell me what the *hell* is going on right now! I just saw a woman jump from an eight-story window. And this crazy guy on the third floor told me to get out. And when I try to call my friends, I just get a busy signal!"

"Of course, my boy. If it'll make you feel better, allow me to explain." He leaned over the front desk, his mouth stretching into a smile. It was only then that I realized there was something wrong with his face. His eyes protruded too far from their sockets, and his lips were so thin, they were barely visible.

"The lift that brought you here," he said, gesturing to the elevator, "travels beyond the veil."

"Are you saying I'm... *dead?*"

"No, no. Well, not exactly. But if you don't find your way back soon, you'll find escape quite impossible, and you may as well be."

"How do I get back? I need to get to Annabelle and Darren–"

He cut me off with a peal of laughter. Shivers crept down my spine. "Why so much concern for *them?*"

"They're my business partners, my friends. My..." The words caught in my throat. "My teammates."

"Are you certain of that?"

I nodded.

"They lied to you."

I balked. "What would you know? I've never met you before in my life. Besides, you're just a... front desk clerk."

"On the contrary, my boy, I know many things." His eyes twinkled, and he leaned forward. A musty, rotten smell came off him, and I cringed. "When you were ten years old, for example, you stole a pack of gum from a shop on 4th Avenue. When you were 18, you were heartbroken when you walked in on your girlfriend–"

"How do you know about that?!" I demanded.

"I have my ways, Kyle. And I'm certain you weren't pulled from the lift by some supernatural force." His bulbous eyes stared me down. His lips curled into an insidious smile. "You were *pushed.*"

My mind raced. I tried to think back to exactly what had happened when I fell onto the third floor. I couldn't recall. One minute, I'd been standing in the elevator. The next, I'd been thrown to the ground.

"It's the human condition, you know. Greed. What did your companions stand to gain by pushing you? Control of the business. Under new management, they can run things how they see fit."

Rage burned within me. I didn't want to believe it, but I knew he was right.

"How do I get back?"

The clerk grinned rapturously, revealing rows of yellowed teeth. "Oh, I'm afraid it's too late for that now."

I turned around. Dark silhouettes filled the lobby. Just like the ones I'd seen on the third floor. Their crimson eyes flashed as they stepped toward me.

"It's been a while since we've had a newcomer," the man behind the desk said, practically salivating in his excitement.

At that moment, against all odds, above the fear and terror, an unexpected courage surged within me.

It's me against this world, I realized. I wasn't going to go out like a coward. Not now, not ever.

I watched the shapes swirl and advance in my direction. Across the dust-covered floors and faded carpet, they came, the very foundation of the hotel quaking beneath their feet. Meanwhile, shadows coalesced on the balconies overhead, watching hungrily.

I was completely surrounded.

I sprinted to the stairwell. The shadows pursued me with superhuman speed, spiraling around the staircase.

*In an effort to lose them, I exited on the third floor and dashed toward the elevator, hoping to reach it before they realized I was no longer on the stairs – but to no avail. The ominous static sound returned. A*s I ran down the hall, *each door I passed swung open w*ith an ear-splitting creak, and the buzzing intensified. Innumerable shadows emerged on both sides, blotting out what little light was available. Their red eyes flared in the darkness.

I came to a halt at the end of the hallway. The shadows swarmed and quickened their pace. Once again, there was no call button on the elevator, but I didn't care. I wedged my fingers between the doors and pushed with all my might.

With a grunt, I forced them open and squeezed into the elevator. As the cacophonous wail of the wraiths reached their crescendo, I pressed the button for the eighth floor. With a shriek, the doors came to a close, mere moments before a horde of outstretched arms arrived.

With a shudder and a groan, the elevator reluctantly ascended. With each second, the din of the screaming specters lessened, until at last they were little more than a gust of wind in the distance. I took a deep breath and did my best to calm down.

My relief was short-lived.

A moment later, the floor shook beneath my feet. I grabbed the railing, as my heart skipped a beat and threatened to evacuate my body. The lights began to flicker. The buttons flashed in a strange, syncopated rhythm.

And then the elevator stopped completely.

Dread settled in the pit of my stomach. *I'm going to be stuck here. Forever.* I ran to the doors and pounded on them, as the lights oscillated madly. "Let me out!" I screamed. "*Let... me... out!*"

Hissing whispers filled the elevator. At first, they were scattered and unintelligible. But then they snapped together, forming one voice.

"Exchange," they said in unison. "We require an exchange."

"Whatever you want!" I screamed. "Anything but me! Just name it!"

"Two," the voices hissed through the static. "We demand two in your stead."

"Yes, yes, fine! Just, please–let me go!"

The elevator trembled.

And then it plummeted.

I screamed the whole way down. I didn't stop until the elevator made impact and the crushing pain consumed me, and everything went black.

***

My eyes fluttered open.

I was lying on something soft. Up above me, light shone from an outdated fixture on the ceiling.

Where am I? I wondered.

I sat up and glanced around. The hallway, the armchair, the bed... I was back in room 812. And across the room, looking out the window, were Annabelle and Darren. Hatred burned within me at the sight of them.

"This must've been the last thing the lady in white saw before she jumped," Annabelle was saying, holding her camcorder. The window was open, and a cool breeze blew inside. They were oblivious to my presence.

"Or, was *pushed*," Darren corrected her.

Silently, I rose from the bed and approached the window. The spirits had demanded an exchange, two in my place. The choice was clear. Darren and Annabelle wouldn't get away with what they'd done.

They'd get what they deserved.

Smiling ear-to-ear, I made my approach. Distracted as they were, my former friends never saw or heard me coming.

Without hesitation, I shoved both of them out the window. Their screams echoed for a second or two before the unforgiving pavement put an end to that.With a smirk, I considered the irony of the situation. Darren and Annabelle would finally get proof of the afterlife—just not in the way they expected.

I walked back over to the bed, picked up the hotel phone, and dialed the front desk. "Hello?" I said, in the most-convincing panicked tone I could muster. "My friends–they just had a terrible accident. They were leaning out of the window, filming, and lost their balance–and–oh my god!" I faked choking sobs. "I think they're dead! Oh my god, they're dead!"

I hung up the phone.

The wintry air swept across my face, as I imagined the whereabouts of the two who had tried to take everything from me.

I grinned.

If room 812 wasn't haunted before... it certainly was now.

THE FLASHLIGHT GAME

Have you ever played "The Flashlight Game"?

I have. And now I will never, ever play it again.

"Okay. Here are the rules," Rachael said, after we'd turned out all the lights. "It's like 'never have I ever,' but with flashlights. Instead of putting a finger down when you've done the thing, you turn off your flashlight. And then... you *hide*."

"So it's like hide-and-seek," I said.

"This sounds dumb," Emma complained.

"Basement's off limits, but everything else is fair game. Sound good?"

We nodded.

It was the summer before ninth grade. The three of us were having a sleepover at Rachael's, and we'd run out of things to do. Her parents were away for the weekend, and her older sister—who was *supposed* to be keeping an eye on us—was at her boyfriend's.

"You start, Ava," Rachael said, pointing to me.

"Okay. Uh..." I glanced at the two of them. Their faces were eerily cast in shadow, as they held the flashlights to their chins. "Never have I ever... been kissed."

Emma clicked her flashlight off. Rachael kept hers on.

"Okay, I'll hide. Count to ten." Emma scrambled up and disappeared into the darkness.

"One, two, three..."

Rachael exchanged an uneasy glance with me. I shrugged and shot her a smile.

"Eight, nine... ten!"

I turned to Rachael. "I heard her go upstairs, right?"

She nodded. We got up, our flashlights shining in the darkness, and started up the stairs. The wood creaked with every step. "She's gonna hear us," Rachael said.

"Don't worry. We'll find her anyway."

And we did. Easily. As soon as we walked into Emma's bedroom, I saw her silhouette, barely peeking out from behind the dresser. "Gotcha!" I yelled, shining the flashlight in her face.

I froze.

There was nothing there.

"What?" I circled the dresser, shining my flashlight all the way behind it—but she wasn't there. I looked back at Rachael. She looked just as confused as I did.

"You saw her there... right?"

"I thought I did. But—but maybe it was just a bit of the wood sticking out, or something." She grabbed my arm and tugged me out of the room. "Come on. Let's check the other rooms."

We walked across the hallway. The door to the bedroom across from us hung open. Quietly, we stepped inside—and my flashlight fell on Emma.

She was crouched right behind the door, grinning madly, her curls wild. "Okay, I lose. Let's play again."

Before I could protest, she pointed at Rachael. "Your turn."

"Fine," she said, shooting a pointed glance at Emma. "Never have I ever... stolen something."

Something flit between them. Rachael glared. Emma sighed, whispered *"fine,"* and clicked off her flashlight.

After a moment's hesitation, I clicked mine off, too. Rachael raised her eyebrows at me in surprise.

Then she began to count.

"One... two..."

Emma grabbed my arm as we ran out of the bedroom. "Did you steal something from Rachael?" I asked in a whisper.

She didn't reply.

"Five... six..."

We crept down the stairs. Emma pulled open the basement door, and dragged me inside.

"Wait—I thought the basement was off-limits—"

"The *basement* is," she said, with a sly smile. "And we're not in the basement."

We stood on a small landing at the top of the stairs. Only a few inches from my feet, the stairs started, descending into the pitch black below.

"Ten!" I heard Rachael faintly call from above.

Emma giggled. "She'll never find us here. We might as well get comfy." She slid down the wall until she was seated on the floor. "So. How's life, Ava?"

I ignored her. "You didn't answer my question earlier. Did you steal something from Rachael?"

"Oh. Pfft." Emma waved her hand dismissively, as though it was a ridiculous question. "Nothing, really."

"She doesn't seem to think it's nothing."

"Yeah, because she's a sensitive little butterfly who can't take a hit."

"You *hit* her?"

"No, that wasn't like, literal. Geez. I meant, she can't take a joke." She glanced over at me. "What did *you* steal?"

My heart pounded. "I, uh... I stole Jenny Harback's gel pens."

"*What?!*" She burst into laughter. "I didn't know you had it in you!"

"I gave them back right after, though. It was too—"

I stopped. Emma wasn't giggling anymore. She was staring past me. Down into the basement.

I turned.

Just in time to see a white light pass by.

"What... what was that?" she whispered.

"I don't know."

"Is someone down there?"

"Rachael's the only one here, and she's out there," I said, backing away from the stairs.

"Maybe it's her older sister. Doesn't her sister sleep down here?"

"I have no idea."

Emma peered down into the darkness. "Hello?" she called down.

"What are you doing? It could be—"

The pitch darkness of the basement slowly illuminated. Then the white light slid back into view. It snapped towards us—and shined in our faces.

We both screamed.

Then we leapt up and scrambled to the door. Emma twisted the handle, yanked on it—but it didn't open. "What the hell?!" she shouted. "Rachael! Rachael, did you lock us in here?!"

I glanced back down.

The flashlight shone up at us from the top of the stairs. Watching.

I couldn't see who was holding it. The light was too bright. "Help!" I screamed. "Open the door!" I grabbed the doorknob, yanked at it madly.

"Rachael! Help!" she screamed.

I glanced back down the stairs.

The light was closer.

It was halfway up the staircase. Twinkling, shimmering, blinding. I could barely make out a hulking silhouette behind it.

"Help!" I screamed. "Please! Rachael—"

The door sprung open.

Rachael slammed it shut behind us, and clicked the deadbolt back into place. "What happened?"

"Someone's down there," Emma gasped, nearly fainting. I just nodded, too terrified to speak.

"Okay. I'll call Mom. Come on."

We walked out to the kitchen, where she called her mom—and then, eventually, the police. But nothing was found in the basement.

Except a flashlight.

A week later, Emma broke down and confessed what she stole. It was a necklace—a gold *R* pendant—that Rachael's father had given her before he left. She ended up returning it. I guess what happened to us that night spooked her into doing the right thing.

But, sometimes, I wonder if that was Rachael's plan all along.

Because, after all—

Who else could have locked the basement door?

OBJECTS IN THE REAR VIEW MIRROR

There's someone in the backseat of my car.

I can't see him. But I can *hear* him. I hear his ragged breaths over the soft tunes of the radio. Hear his soft words whispered in my ear.

I feel him, too. I feel him pressing his hands against the back of my seat, as if he can feel my body through them. I feel the shift in air as he moves his head close to mine. Feel his fingertips as he brushes my neck.

But all I can do is keep driving.

My plan was to drive all night from Tulsa, Oklahoma to Lancaster, California. My hometown. Where my wedding is to take place in two days.

The drive started out well. The car is a rental from a family friend, Mr. Craggs, and it rode incredibly smooth. I put in a Journey CD, turned the volume up, and coasted through the darkness. The flat sand of the Mohave desert extended in all directions around me, under the purple sky.

My mind was filled with thoughts of the wedding. I couldn't wait to marry the love of my life, Enrico… but I also carried a heaviness in my heart. Because my hometown did not hold happy memories for me. My parents had twisted my arm, begging me to hold it there, so our frugal relatives could all attend.

Now I regretted that choice.

I was driving through the Mohave desert around 4 AM when I first heard his voice.

"Rebecca."

My entire body froze.

The voice was a whisper on the wind. Barely audible over the guitar chords, the beats of the drum. *Must've been my imagination.* I turned up the music and focused on the open road in front of me.

Then I heard it again.

"Rebecca."

The car swerved underneath me. I stomped on the brakes. It came to a halt on the shoulder, next to a cluster of Joshua trees.

Heart pounding in my chest, I wheeled around.

The backseat was empty.

"I'm okay. I'm okay." I took a deep, shuddering breath, and turned on the interior lights just to make sure it was empty. I even climbed halfway back there, peering at the blind spot behind my seat, making sure no one was crouched there. Even though, logically, I knew they couldn't fit.

My heart finally slowed. I turned out the lights, turned up the radio, and pulled back out onto the main road.

That's when I heard his voice again.

"Made you look."

My whole body froze. I glanced in the rearview mirror—yet again, the backseat was empty. All I could see were the black cloth seats, the rear window that looked out at the desert sky.

"You're going crazy, Rebecca. The stress is getting to you," I told myself. It was true—in the last few days, I'd probably averaged about four hours of sleep a night. There were so many last-minute things to do. Namecards, favors, and rearranging the seating arrangement because a few people had cancelled last minute.

That's when I felt a hot gust of air on my neck.

I yelped in surprise. The car swerved madly all over the road; cacti and endless hills of sand flashed in the headlights. "Who's there?!" I screamed.

"You know who I am, Rebecca."

The voice *was* familiar. I hadn't heard it in several years. I'd tried to scrub it from my memory entirely. Along with every other memory of him.

"Alex?"

The voice laughed behind me, almost in my ear. "Did you miss me?" he said, coolly.

I glanced at the rearview mirror again. Empty.

"You're not real."

"I'm talking to you, aren't I?"

"You're dead," I stuttered.

"Correction. I killed myself, after you broke up with me," the voice answered behind me. "But you don't like to hear that, do you?"

I drove in silence, knuckles white against the steering wheel. I tried to focus on the passing cacti. Saguaro rose up on either side, reaching up to the moon with their needled arms. Like men begging for their prayers to be answered.

"I didn't... I never wanted you to die," I said into the silence. "I just didn't want to be with you anymore. I didn't mean—"

"You should've known what that would do. I told you I couldn't live without you."

"But—"

"You said you wanted to marry me. To be my wife."

"I was seventeen!" I screamed, tears burning my eyes. "I had no idea what I wanted! And that was before—before—"

"Before what?"

Before the night at the lake house. Before I got drunk for the very first time. Before I felt your hands climbing up my legs. Before I stared blankly at the ugly light fixture on the ceiling, spinning around and around, unsure what exactly was happening.

"Before you took what was mine."

A beat of silence. The wind roared in my ears, the tires rolled furiously across the road.

Then, he growled in my ear: "You liked it."

"No, I didn't!" I screamed. "And if—if I hadn't been drinking—I would have forced you away, and—"

I stopped.

Something wet and warm trailed up the side of my neck. His tongue.

I whipped around in my seat.

It was empty.

I took in a deep, shuddering breath. Kept my eyes locked on the road in front of me, the desert hills, the cacti, the red rocks. "You have no control over me, anymore," I said quietly. "I won't listen to your lies. Back then, I was young and stupid. I'm not anymore. I'm about to get married."

"You think your husband-to-be is any different from me?" His voice came out low and soft—now directly behind me. "We're all the same underneath, Rebecca."

I felt his hands press into the back of the seat, against the small of my back. I leaned forward, heart pounding in my chest.

"No. He's different."

"Do you really believe that?"

I glanced into the rearview mirror. My heart plummeted. This time, there was a silhouette in the shadows. Blocking out the stars through the back window.

"Yes. I do," I said, my voice trembling. "He would never do what you did to me. He's a good man."

"You thought I was a good man once, too."

My blood turned to ice. That was true. Once I thought the world of Alex, and my entire world revolved around him. But I was young and stupid then. "He's a good man," I repeated.

A soft laugh from the backseat.

"We're all the same, Rebecca. So why not be with me? You loved me, didn't you?"

"No—I—"

"We were meant to be together, forever."

Cold fingers crept over my shoulders, then down my arms. I felt them interlock with my fingers, even though I couldn't see anything.

"And now we will be."

He tugged at my hands.

The steering wheel slipped.

The car swerved. Then it careened off the road, flying over rocks and sand. I screamed. I stomped on the break, and the car spun, kicking up sand.

"Stop!" I screamed.

The car halted to a stop. My whole body jerked forward. My head smacked against the steering wheel. Pain flooded my head.

Then: silence.

With a gasping breath, I pulled myself up. I didn't look in the back seat. Instead, I put the pedal to the floor, raced over the sand, and turned back onto the road.

I expected his voice to start up again—but there was only silence.

For several minutes, I kept my eyes locked on the road, praying the silence would continue. When it did, I gathered the courage to glance in the rearview mirror.

The back seat was empty.

And through the window, the first light of dawn was breaking across the horizon. Streaks of orange and pink, framed by the golden sand that stretched out in every direction. The darkness receded, giving way to fire, to light, to day.

Tomorrow, I would be married.

And I was finally ready.

FIT RUNNING BUDDY

I got a new fitness app.

I'm in terrible shape. I run, like, 12-minute miles. Thankfully, this new app—"FitRunningBuddy"—claims to turn even the laziest of couch potatoes into fast runners. They even had a guarantee: *If you don't run an 8-minute mile in your first month, get your money back!*

When I downloaded it, it asked for all the usual info. Name, height, weight. Access to my location so that it could log my distance, calculate my speed. Then it popped up with its first notification:

Please schedule your first run! :)

I typed *8 PM Wednesday.* I'd do an evening run after work to burn off some of my dinner calories.

Thank you! We've scheduled your run. :)

When Wednesday came, the app gave me notifications throughout the day. At 4 PM: *remember, Bethany, your run is tonight at 8 PM!*

I dismissed the notification.

But I got another one at 5 PM. And at 6 PM. In fact, I got one every hour—until 7:30 PM, when they came in every five minutes. *Ping!* **Are you ready for your run?** *Ping!* **Get pumped! Your run starts in fifteen minutes! :)**

At that point, I was pretty annoyed. But then, I laughed, as I realized—that's probably why the app is so damn effective. *Even the worst of us will get so irritated by the constant notifications, we'll go running just to shut the damn thing up.*

At 7:55 PM, I pulled my old sneakers out of the closet. Then I put on my favorite playlist, put in my earbuds, and stepped out onto the sidewalk.

I ran down my street, took a left, and entered the park. It's usually desolate in the evening—but, tonight, there was a man sitting on the bench. He looked up at me and smiled.

I forced a smile back—despite feeling awfully self-conscious about how slow I was going, how heavy I was breathing.

The first few minutes of the run went well. I'd made it halfway around the pond, and I didn't quite feel like dying yet. That was good. Really good.

Then I got that prickly feeling on the back of my neck.

You know the feeling. It's like every muscle, every cell, in your body is screaming *someone is watching you! Turn around, you idiot!* Yeah, well, I *was* an idiot this time—and ignored it. Because every cell in my body was also screaming *stop and sit down. Walk home. Eat some ice cream. You earned it.*

Then, seconds later, I heard a distinct *thump* behind me.

I yanked out my earbuds and whipped around.

My heart stopped.

A man stood behind me. The same man that had smiled at me on the bench. Now, he watched me with a different smile. A predatory, wolfish smile. Eyes taking in every inch of my body.

Heart pounding, I picked up my pace.

So did he.

He broke into a run. And he was *fast*. In seconds, he'd closed half the gap between us.

I broke into a sprint, my tired legs pumping as fast as they could. *No. No. Please, no.* I whipped around—the man was only several feet from me, now.

And something silver glinted in his right hand.

"Get away from me!" I screamed, pushing myself faster. My legs ached, my lungs burned, my vision blurred with tears. I felt like I was dying.

I glanced back.

He's right behind me.

I could feel his hot breath on his neck. Feel the air shift from his movements behind me.

No. Please, no, no.

I saw the exit to the park up ahead. Skin prickling, fire spreading through my muscles, I forced myself forward.

Something cold and sharp pressed against my back.

I screamed.

Then, as soon as I felt it—it disappeared. I ran like the wind, stumbling over my feet, until I flew through the park's exit. Then I glanced back.

The man had stopped. He just stood there, on the sidewalk. No longer chasing. Just watching.

At that exact moment, my phone pinged.

With a notification from *FitRunningBuddy*.

Congratulations! Your time for running your mile is: 7:47. We hope you enjoyed the experience! :)

Please schedule your next run now.

FIGURE OF SPEECH

It all started on a Wednesday.

I was getting ready for work downstairs, trying to brush the huge tangle out of my hair. "Hey, David? I'll pick up your suit on the way home!" I shouted up the stairs.

"Oh, you don't have to!" David shouted back.

"The dry cleaner's right on the way. Kill two birds with one stone." With that, I yanked the brush through my hair, grabbed my purse, and stepped out the door.

I froze.

In the middle of the sidewalk were two dead birds. Gray feathers matted with blood. Mouths open. Eyes staring blankly at the sky.

Several inches from their heads was a large rock.

"David?" I called up the stairs. "There are some dead birds out here! Can you come get them?"

It was a big ask. But I *was* getting his suit, so we were even.

Probably.

David shuffled out, carrying a plastic bag. Turning it inside-out, he crouched and picked up the birds. "They flew into the window again, huh?" he asked.

I glanced at the rock. It had a small patch of blood on it—and a gray feather. "I think they hit the rock, actually."

"I'll never understand birds. Smart enough to migrate hundreds of miles, but dumb enough to fly right into glass. Or a rock." He shook his head. "Birds are *weird*, aren't they?"

"Ha, you can say that again."

The instant I said it, his face went completely slack. His eyes lost focus. The bag slipped from his hands. And he repeated, in monotone: "I'll never understand birds. Smart enough to migrate hundreds of miles, but dumb enough to fly right into glass. Or a—"

"David. I heard you the first time."

"Oh, I know!" he said cheerily. As if he weren't acting like a total weirdo. Then he looked down, finally noticing he dropped the bag. "Whoops, dropped it."

He picked up the birds and disappeared back inside.

I didn't make the connection right away. With this whole bird fiasco, I was late for work, now. A hundred students would be waiting for me to teach them MECH 203: Introduction to Robotics. Probably hungover students who were also late, but still.

I ran down the halls of the engineering building. When I got inside, most of my class was there. The lecture got off to a rocky start, but wasn't a disaster.

"Remember, problem set 6 is due on Friday!" I said, as the students filed out. "And office hours start now."

Class dismissed. I made my way to my office, sat down, and began peeling an orange.

"Professor Sandling?"

I looked up to see Evan McDonnell enter my office. The worst student in my entire class. "Hi, Evan," I said, barely able to conceal my disdain.

He handed me a stack of paper.

"What's this?"

"Problem set 5."

I raised an eyebrow. "This was due a *week* ago."

"I told you, I needed extra time. I'm the event planner for our fraternity and we had a *huge* thing last week. I emailed you about an extension—"

"That I didn't grant!"

"Please, Professor Sandling?"

"No. You're too late."

"But—I *need* to pass this class. I promise I'll get everything else in on time. It won't happen again. I promise."

I hesitated. This guy was a total goof off, but he seemed earnest this time. Some kids were only pushed into action when the threat of failure loomed over their heads. "You can do an extra credit assignment. Due two days from now."

"Oh, no, I can't hand in something that soon. I—"

"Oh, come on! Put your money where your mouth is!"

His eyes widened.

Then he began to retch. Violently. Choking, coughing sounds filled the room. His body convulsed madly.

"Evan! Are you okay?!"

He didn't reply. The chair slid out from under him—he bent over on the tiled floor—retching, shaking.

"I'm—I'm going to call 911," I said. I grabbed my phone and started dialing as he convulsed on the floor.

"What is your emergency?"

"One of my students just started coughing and retching, and he's collapsed on the floor. And—"

Plink.

Something shot out of his mouth and hit the floor.

A penny.

We both stared at it. He looked at me, shuddering, his face pale.

"Are you okay?"

"Yeah, I think so," he replied, his voice hoarse. "I'm... I'm going to go back to my dorm."

Then he was gone.

I stared at the penny, every muscle in my body frozen. *Put your money where your mouth is. You can say that again. Kill two birds with one stone.*

All of them, within seconds, came true.

I opened my mouth. Heart pounding in my chest, I said, hesitantly:

"Time flies... when you're... having fun?"

In the blink of an eye, the windows behind me darkened.

I whipped around. It was night outside. Complete with twinkling stars and a full moon. When it had been morning *seconds* before.

I glanced at my phone.

1:17 AM

13 missed calls

"What the hell?"

I ran out to the parking lot as fast as my feet would take me. "David, I'm so sorry," I said into the phone, as I started the car. "I was helping a student and I—I didn't realize how much time had gone by."

When I got in the door, David hugged me and wouldn't let go. "I thought something terrible had happened to you," he said, nearly crying with happiness. "When you didn't come home... I..."

"I'm so, so sorry. I had a meeting with a student, and then I started grading exams, and I didn't realize it had gotten so late."

A flimsy excuse. But David was so happy to see me, he didn't ask any questions. He just held me tight and wouldn't let go.

Days passed. I tried to forget about my little problem. I chose my words carefully, and I didn't have any disasters. The worst was when I told David I was *feeling under the weather,* and suddenly a horrible tempest blew in, raining down on our little house.

Then Thursday came. This was a special class for MECH 203—I was bringing in an *actual robot.* I couldn't wait to see the looks on their faces when I showed them how the robot could climb stairs.

"This robot is only six-inches high," I said, as hundreds of eyes stared back at me. "But with clever engineering, it will climb these stairs." I placed the robot at the base of the stairs leading back up through the lecture hall. My finger poised on the button, I said proudly to the class:

"This'll blow your mind!"

I clapped my hand over my mouth.

But it was too late.

Read more scary stories at:
www.blair-daniels.com

Get the first book at: http://geni.us/DontScream

Get *Shadow on the Stairs* at: http://geni.us/Shadow

Made in the USA
Las Vegas, NV
14 August 2024

93838280R00156